I0674938

The Rabbi's Sex Class

RABBI MICHAEL GOLD

Paper back ISBN-13: 978-1-946469-29-8
Hardcover ISBN-13: 978-1-946469-30-4

ShelteringTree.Earth, LLC Publishing
PO Box 973, Eagle Lake, FL 33839

ShelteringTree.Earth

Did you enjoy this book?
We love to hear from our readers.
Please email the author at MGold@ShelteringTree.Earth
or write to the author at the address above.

DEDICATION

To all my students, both in my congregation, in the colleges where
I teach, and around the country. As Rabbi Hanina says in the
Talmud (*Taanit* 7a):

אָמַר רַבִּי חֲנִינָא : הַרְבֵּה לָמַדְתִּי מֵרַבּוֹתַי, וּמֵחֲבֵירַי
יוֹתֵר מֵרַבּוֹתַי, וּמִתַּלְמִידַי יוֹתֵר מִכּוּלָן.

"Rabbi Hanina said, I have learned much from my teachers, more
from my colleagues, and most from my students."

MICHAEL GOLD

CONTENTS

ACKNOWLEDGEMENTS

The Jewish Publication Society of America published my book *Does God Belong in the Bedroom?* in 1992. It was an honor to be published by such a prestigious Jewish publishing house. As a result of the book, I had the opportunity of lecturing on Jewish sexual ethics throughout the United States as well as Europe and Mexico. I was also privileged to serve as the co-chair of the Rabbinical Assembly special committee on sexual ethics. I want to thank my editor at the time Ellen Frankel, now Editor Emeritus of the Jewish Publication Society.

In *Does God Belong in the Bedroom?,* my goal was to present a view of Jewish sexual ethics in terms of gray rather than black and white, forbidden and permitted. I see a continuum of sexual behavior, what I call a ladder of holiness. On the bottom of the ladder is unethical sex. In the middle of the ladder is sex which may be ethical but falls short of the Jewish ideal of holiness. The goal is to climb the ladder towards sex that fulfills the Jewish idea of holiness.

As the years went by, my views on sexuality evolved. This became clear as my children entered adulthood and left home. Perhaps the biggest change for me personally was the decision under certain conditions to perform lesbian and gay weddings. I thought about rewriting my original book. But my wife Evelyn, always filled with wisdom and insight, wanted me to write fiction. I want to thank Evelyn for her love and support during 43 years of marriage.

Could a book on Jewish sexual ethics be written as a novel? Over the years I have taught the teens from my synagogue at our local Jewish high school. I always included lessons on Jewish sexual ethics for these students. My thought was that a rabbi was the best source to teach these young people proper sexual behavior. These lessons to my teens gave me the idea to write this book.

As I approached retirement from a busy synagogue in suburban Fort Lauderdale, my congregation went on lockdown during Covid. All services were conducted online. I finally had the time to work on this novel.

Perhaps it was serendipity that Evelyn Rainey of ShelteringTree.Earth LLC Publishing sent out an email to religion professors searching for manuscripts on religious themes. I sent her my manuscript and a match was made. She is my editor and publisher, going over my book with a fine-tooth comb to help me perfect it. I appreciate her faith in me and my book.

Rabbi Michael Gold

MICHAEL GOLD

PROLOGUE

If I had known that teaching a class on sexual ethics at a suburban Jewish parochial school would cost me my job as a rabbi, I never would have volunteered. What could be the downside? A rabbi teaching a group of high school students, many from his own synagogue, about sexual behavior, seemed like a good idea. Where else would they learn right and wrong? From their friends? From the internet? From social media? Everyone tried to talk me out of it. The school. My synagogue. Even my wife. But I persisted, feeling this was important. And that is how the trouble started.

I had approached the school in the late spring about teaching in the fall. It was a hot afternoon in late May when Dr. Judith Baker invited me into her booklined office. A thin woman with a deep scowl, she had made the school one of the best college preparatory private schools in the state. However, although it was called the Eastman Jewish Academy, the school was not Jewish enough for my taste. Still, my son Joshua was a senior and my daughter Shira was a freshman there. If I wanted a Jewish secondary education without the extreme Orthodoxy of Chabad, it was the only reasonable choice.

"Come in, Rabbi Williams," she said, in a voice that seemed cold, as if she was too busy to see me.

"Please call me Efraim," I responded.

"I am not the most religious woman in the world, but I find it hard to call a rabbi by his first name. Tell me, what is this about a sex class?"

Wisdom said that this woman did not want to waste time with small talk. "Dr. Baker, I want to offer to teach a weekly class in your school on sexual ethics. I want to seriously study how Judaism views sexuality."

"Rabbi, we have a teacher of Judaism."

I thought about the black coated, black hat rabbi who taught Judaism to these students. He was popular with the students. "Rabbi Lebovic is a good man. I know him. But he works for the Israel Outreach Center, whose goal is to convince Jews to return to an Orthodox lifestyle. His views on sexual ethics reflect the world he comes from. Not only no sex outside marriage, but no physical contact before marriage. Early marriage shortly after the age of eighteen, often arranged. Strict laws of sexual contact even within marriage. Homosexuality is forbidden. Masturbation is forbidden. These are average American teenagers. They hang out, they hook up, in school I know they wear uniforms, but outside of school they dress in the most provocative way. They need a more liberal view of sex in keeping with Jewish values."

"They learn about sex in their health class."

"I am not talking about the biology of sex. I know they learn about the birds and the bees. But do they learn how to say *no*. I am talking about the ethics of sex. What is right and what is wrong, from a more liberal Jewish point of view."

Dr. Baker rattled the papers on her desk. "Rabbi Williams, you know how tight the budget is. The school is barely keeping its head above water. I cannot afford another teacher, even once a week."

I thought about the tuition we pay each year for our two children. Over $30,000 a year. From kindergarten to twelfth grade there were close to 300 students, with parents paying that kind of tuition. The school could not be that broke. "Dr. Baker, I am not worried about the money. I will do this as a volunteer."

"I am not sure the officers of the school will go for it."

It was time for me to exert some of my authority. "I am the rabbi of the largest non-Orthodox synagogue in the area. I officiated at the bar and bat mitzvah of probably half your students. They see me as their rabbi. I want them to learn Jewish values from their rabbi."

Dr. Baker leaned forward, and her voice softened, as if she did not want anyone outside to hear. "Rabbi, let me be totally honest with you. You might not want to hear this. You're a rabbi after all. Most of the parents who send their children to this school are not particularly interested in Judaism. Yes, they want their children to read Hebrew, support Israel, come to synagogue on the high holidays, and hopefully marry a Jew someday. But they do not want too much Judaism. If a child comes home from our school and tells his or her parents they want to keep kosher, I get complaints. *We did not send our child there to become a rabbi!* I am not sure the parents will go for it."

She continued, "Do you know why the vast majority of parents send their children to this school? They want them to get into a good college. We have the highest number of graduates going to Ivy League schools of any private school in the state. We prepare our graduates for the best universities. That is what is important to our parents. I might say that that is their religion. Learning a Jewish view of sex is not important to them." What she told me was no surprise, although it was unusual for a school administrator to say it so bluntly.

"Dr. Baker, these students who go off to these excellent colleges will feel pressure to hook up, to have sex, to sext on-line. Some will be bullied by other students, often over sexual issues. They will hear comments about their bodies, and they will often be made to feel inadequate. They are not going to be able to deal with these issues by what they learn in a health class. And they will not be able to deal with these issues after a class taught by an ultra-Orthodox rabbi. They need a modern view of sexual ethics."

She took a deep breath and leaned back. "Rabbi, I see your point. But I will have to discuss it with my education committee and my officers. I will get back to you." She stood up and held out her hand. I was being dismissed.

I did hear back from her several days later. "Rabbi Williams, you can teach your class every other Monday afternoon. It will be one hour, the last class of the day."

"Why every other week? I was hoping for every week."

"Rabbi Lebovic is teaching an advanced Talmud class every other week. He also wanted every week. He was not happy when I told him that his class would flipflop with your class."

She continued, "The officers of the school said it could only be open to seniors." Good, I thought, my son will be in it. "One more thing. Students can only attend your class with written permission of their parents."

I was a bit taken aback. "Do your students need permission to attend Rabbi Lebovic's classes?"

Her voice was stern, "He is our regular Judaica teacher. Parents know about him when they sign up their children to attend our school. You are an outsider, and you are teaching a very controversial topic. I want parental permission."

My next job was to convince my synagogue, or at least the officers of my synagogue. I met Barry Pollack at a posh club downtown. Barry, partner in a major law firm, certainly belonged to the club, as did other lawyers, doctors, businessmen. Women were not welcome until recently when a local city commissioner, a woman, threatened a lawsuit.

The seats were plush, and the dining room walls shone with beautifully stained wood. I wore a suit, something that I rarely did these days except on Shabbat and for funerals and weddings. But a jacket for men was the norm in this place. Barry was a big man and a powerful presence. I would not want to face him in a courtroom, litigating for his client. But in his two terms as my synagogue president, he and I had learned to work together. I believe a big part of that was how I had handled his daughter Miriam's bat mitzvah. A delicate girl, very pretty but very shy; I had helped her chant a *haftarah* and deliver a speech with confidence. It dawned on me as I shook hands with Barry that Miriam Pollack was a senior, and if her parents approved, she would also be in my class.

"Rabbi, they have lobster on the lunch menu today. I know you won't eat it, but do you mind if I order it?"

I always wondered what would make someone eating lunch with their rabbi order the most blatantly unkosher item on the menu. "Do what you want." He ordered the lobster rolls, and I ordered a piece of grilled salmon on a Caesar salad. Barry had also ordered a bottle of expensive white wine, pouring me a glass without asking me.

"So, tell me what you are planning."

I told him of my plans to teach a class in sexual ethics at the Eastman Jewish Academy. I mentioned how students needed the guidance in this area that Jewish tradition could provide. I spoke about students hooking up, teen-age depression and suicide, often tied to sexual issues, homosexuality and the difficulty of gays admitting their preferences. He listened carefully, until I realized I was talking too much; I shut up.

"Rabbi, I like you. We work well together. But as president of the synagogue, I am responsible to the board. Will it hurt the synagogue's reputation to have its rabbi speaking to teens about such personal topics? Will we gain members or lose members if you go ahead? In truth, I worry that we will lose members. You will become known as *the sex rabbi*. I know our people. Some will even say that you are influencing our kids to have sex at too young an age. Have you thought about the effect on our congregation?"

"Barry, in all honesty I think they will be proud of their rabbi. They will say that our rabbi can talk to teenagers about a very personal, vital issue."

Barry leaned forward and lowered his voice. The bluster diminished. For one moment, he seemed almost meek. "Rabbi Williams, I want to share something with you. But first I must know if what I tell you is confidential."

"It is part of my job to keep confidences."

"Rabbi, I know that. I have been keeping this a secret, just me and my wife. But it is troubling me. You know my daughter Miriam -the sweet timid girl you bat mitzvahed four years ago. This year she will become a senior at Eastman."

I wanted to tell him that bat mitzah is not a verb; I do not bat mitzvah people. But I kept silent.

He continued in a somber tone, "Last month I came home early from work. I heard a noise from her bedroom. Miriam has been seeing this college kid, Kevin. I don't like him. My wife doesn't like him. There were Miriam and Kevin, lying in bed. He was in his underwear and she was in panties and bra, nothing else. I did not see them in the act, but I am sure that a few minutes later they would have done it. I immediately threw Kevin out of the house. He could not get his pants on fast enough. I told Miriam to wait in her room. I would be back to talk to her shortly. I needed time to cool down. Imagine him taking advantage of my daughter in my own house."

I did not want to say that it sounded like his daughter was a willing participant.

"Well, I went back to her room a half hour later. The window was open, and she was gone. I don't know where she went, I assume to meet him. I decided not to call her. I heard her sneak in late that night. She thought I was asleep. I decided to wait another day. When I did confront her, she spoke back harshly. *Dad, I am seventeen years old. I am no longer a little girl. I am old enough to make my own decisions about who I see and what I do. I love Kevin. You and Mom cannot tell me what to do.* I shouted at her, *As long as you live under our roof you will obey our rules. Kevin is not welcome here.*"

Some heads were turning towards us, so I gestured him to lower his voice.

"Sorry. Rabbi, I immediately regretted the harshness of my words. She was not wrong. At seventeen, I cannot control her. I am worried about my little girl. I believe she is sexually active, and I am worried that she will be hurt by this boy, or worse, become pregnant. Rabbi, I want you to teach that class. I want my daughter in that class. Maybe you will talk some sense into her, into all of these kids. Maybe you can convince them that high school students are too young for sex."

I answered, "I wish I had such influence. But I will try." I knew that he had shared something deep and painful. His little girl was growing up. He could not keep her in a protective bubble. Perhaps she had made a mistake, and she would continue to make more mistakes. It is a truth that every parent knows.

We finished the meal with small talk about the petty reality of synagogue politics, as Barry signed for the lunch.

There was one more person I had to convince to allow me to teach the class. I knew that Marcia would be the toughest sell of all. We had been married twenty-one years, had two teenage children, yet she still looked like the pretty college sophomore I met at a Shabbat dinner at Colombia University Hillel. At that time, she was studying psychology and exploring her Jewish roots. I was already a seminary student. My eyes were immediately drawn to her. Today she was the office manager of a large medical practice, the only person who could keep the multiple egos of the various doctors in check.

As well as being a mom and a career woman, Marcia was focused on my career. She seemed to know what I needed in order to keep my career on track. She told me if I was not dressing sharp enough, if my sermons were boring, if I had neglected someone in the hospital or an elderly shut-in. She knew before I did if a board member was planning to bring me down, and she had the ability to invite the right people over for Shabbat dinner to keep my career in line. Without her, I would not have been as successful a rabbi. I needed her approval if I were to teach this class.

I spoke directly over dinner, one evening when the kids were out with friends. "Marcia, I am planning to teach a class at Eastman for seniors. Joshua will be in the class. It will be a class in sexual ethics."

Marcia paused. I sensed that she already knew my plans before I mentioned anything. She was calculating how this would affect my career. "Why?"

"They are learning about sex from the internet, from social media, from their friends. Let them learn about sexual values from their rabbi."

"Efraim, do you really understand the world these kids live in? You and I grew up during the sexual revolution. We were not shy about experimenting with sex. But these kids. To them, sex is about hooking up. It is recreational, with no further meaning. What makes you think they will listen to you?"

"Marcia, I see what is happening. I watch the movies and television. People casually hopping into bed with each other. And as a result, teen pregnancy is up, abortion is us, sexting and sexual bullying are up. Maybe, just maybe I can make a difference."

"So, you will speak to our teenagers about homosexuality, about abortion, about masturbation. What will that do to your reputation in the community? It could cost you your job."

In hindsight, I realize how close she was to being correct.

Marcia switched gears. "Efraim, if you teach this class, I want you to promise me something. I know you like to talk about us, about how our family lives our Jewish lives. You must promise me that you will never mention anything about you and me, about our sexual lives. You and I need to have a wall of privacy around our personal lives."

"Do you think I am Rav Kahane?"

"Who is Rav Kahane?"

"The Talmud tells a story of how Rav Kahane, as a young rabbinical student, hid under the bed of his rabbi. He listened as the rabbi made love with his wife. Feeling that his rabbi was being too immodest, he came out from under the bed and criticized him. *You would think the master never sipped the cup before.* His rabbi said, *Kahane, it is rude. You need to leave.* Kahane answered, *This too is Torah. I have come to learn.*"

Marcia chuckled, "That is really in the Talmud? I will have to check under that bed before we fool around."

"Marcia, I promise that I will respect our realm of privacy. In fact, one of the first lessons I want to teach these young people is the importance of privacy." And so, I received my wife's reluctant permission. The class was starting in September. I needed to outline the material I wanted to share with my students.

1. THE FRIDAY NIGHT PARTY

"Are you taking the rabbi's sex class?" Isar Amir took a bite of his hamburger and looked at his friend Joshua. Isar was taller and huskier than Joshua, outweighing him by a good thirty pounds. In a public high school, he might have played on the football team. Here, in the Eastman Jewish Academy, they only offered flag football. Joshua and Isar had been best friends since childhood.

Friday was a meat day in the school cafeteria. The trays carrying the greasy hamburgers were red, a sign that only a kosher meat meal could touch the tray. Monday, Wednesday, and Fridays were meat days. Tuesdays and Thursdays were dairy days. Students could bring their lunch from home any day, but they had to follow the same rules. Most of the seniors ignored it.

The seniors tended to eat at the far side of the cafeteria, separated from the younger students. Non-seniors were not welcome, unless there was a younger girlfriend of a senior boy. No senior girl would have a younger boyfriend.

"Do I have a choice about taking the class?" Joshua

responded. "My dad is teaching it. Who wants to learn about sex from a class taught by their dad?" Although Joshua already knew what his friend would say, he asked him, "Are you taking the class?"

"My dad won't let me take it. He said if I want to learn about sex and Judaism, I should study with a real rabbi."

Joshua had heard this from his friend for years. Isar's dad was Israeli. To him, a real rabbi had a black coat, a black beard, and fringes hanging outside, the kind of rabbis they had in Israel. Rabbi Lebovic was a real rabbi. Isar's dad, in his gruff Israeli manner, loved to put down Rabbi Williams. *What kind of rabbi drives on Shabbat, lets women be called to the Torah, even performs weddings between two men?* His father had never performed a gay wedding; if he had, Joshua would have heard. But that didn't stop Isar's father from saying it was so.

Isar continued. "My dad absolutely forbade it. He says that I can go to study hall during class. He said maybe a little bit of extra studying would do me some good."

Over the years, Joshua had defended his dad to Isar's family. His dad kept kosher, observed the Sabbath, driving only to synagogue and back, and prayed with *tefillin* every day. From what he saw, Isar's family was not observant, going to synagogue only on the holiest days of the year. But the only synagogue they would attend had an Orthodox rabbi. Isar and Joshua had come to a kind of agreement about whether Joshua's dad was a *real rabbi*. Isar had enjoyed many a Shabbat dinner at the Williams' home. He knew that some day when he married, he would probably ask Rabbi

Williams to perform the wedding, assuming he married a Jew. But for the moment he had to accept his dad's opinion that Joshua's father was not a *real rabbi*.

"Give me a report on what you learn in class. Do you think he will teach the proper way to whack off?"

Joshua punched his shoulder, not enough to hurt but enough to make a point. "I doubt that the school will let my dad talk about masturbation. It is not something good Jewish boys are supposed to do."

Isar answered. "There are two kinds of Jews in the world. Those who masturbate and admit it, and those who masturbate and don't admit it."

Joshua replied, "I will give you a full report after study hall. The word among the seniors is that four or five of them are not allowed in the class by their parents. I wonder if these parents think, if their kids talk about sex, they will try sex."

David Eisenberg walked over to the two boys. He looked at the hamburgers they were eating and said, "You two are still killing animals for food." David was slight, almost delicate looking. He opened a sack lunch and took out a cheese sandwich.

"Hey, it's a meat day. You are not allowed to eat that."

"What are they going to do, not let me graduate? Don't worry, I won't let any cheese touch your precious hamburgers." When they were younger, the teachers used to monitor what students brought from home. If they brought dairy on a meat day or meat on a dairy day, or any kind of non-kosher meat, the teachers would confiscate their lunch. But now that they were seniors, the faculty preferred to leave them alone. One teacher stood at the far side of the cafeteria, near the younger kids, ignoring the seniors. David took a bite of his sandwich. "I need protein, and I am not going to get it by killing animals."

"No, you will get it by keeping cows locked up and stealing their milk," Isar said cynically. David had been a vegetarian for less than a year. The other boys loved to tease him about it.

Joshua decided to change the subject. "Are you taking my dad's sex class?"

"My parents want me to take it…"

Isar interrupted. "I guess your parents are hoping that the class will make you straight."

"You can't take a gay and make him straight." David's classmates had suspected for several years that he was gay. They had noted his silence when they talked about girls. Now he seemed much more concerned with his looks than ever before. Perhaps that was part of his new embrace of vegetarianism. Finally, during the summer, David revealed himself to his parents. His mom seemed to accept it, but his dad started to cry. It was only the second time David had seen his father cry, the first was at his grandmother's funeral. David had hugged both his parents, and said, "Mom, Dad, it is who I am."

Isar continued, "You know Rabbi Williams is going to talk about homosexuality to the class. That from a rabbi who performs gay marriages."

Joshua immediately defended his father. "You don't know if my dad performs gay marriages."

David spoke in a serious tone. "My dad used to be on the board of that synagogue. He was very upset when he found out I was gay. If the synagogue found out that Rabbi Williams was performing gay marriages, they would probably fire him. There are some very traditional people on that board. Personally, I think if he did perform gay marriages, that would be a wonderful thing."

"Why, are you getting married?" Isar teased David. He knew that David was not in a relationship. At that moment, the boys saw Miriam and Katy walking in their direction with hamburgers on their trays. Isar motioned them to come join them.

Miriam Pollack and Katy Roberts had been best friends since the year they became bat mitzvah. They did everything together. As the years had gone by, Katy felt more and more inadequate around Miriam. Miriam, the slight, shy girl at her bat mitzvah, had grown beautiful. She still had her slim figure but was perfectly proportioned, with gorgeous blue eyes. Katy was a bit jealous of Miriam's college boyfriend Kevin, even if Miriam's father forbade her from seeing him. Miriam always found ways to sneak out and be with Kevin.

When Katy was with Miriam, she kept thinking of the story in the Bible of the two sisters Leah and Rachel. The older sister Leah had soft eyes, while Rachel was beautiful and comely. Jacob had fallen in love with the beautiful Rachel and been forced to marry the soft eyed Leah. In Katy's mind, Miriam was Rachel, and she was Leah. She didn't know if she had soft eyes, but her brown eyes and brown stringy hair made her plain looking. On top of that, she felt chunky next to Miriam's slim body. She went to the gym several days a week but could never seem to lose the weight around her hips. If the Eastman Jewish Academy had allowed cheerleaders, Miriam would have been the head cheerleader; Katy would probably handle the equipment in the locker room. Miriam, to her credit, was a sincere friend who never commented about Katy's looks.

Katy and Miriam sat next to the three boys. Miriam, besides her hamburger, had taken a large plate of French fries. Katy had resisted the fries and wondered how Miriam could eat anything she wanted and stay so slim. The moment they sat down, Isar reached his hand over and helped himself to several fries. "You don't mind, Miriam." She merely smiled.

Isar continued, "Are you two taking Rabbi William's sex class?"

Miriam responded, "My dad did not give me any choice. My parents never discussed sex with me at all. It was a forbidden topic. Now suddenly, since I began dating Kevin, he is worried that I will get pregnant. He could not wait to sign that permission paper."

Katy looked at her and then said, "I am not worried about getting pregnant. You have to have a boyfriend first. But I am taking the class." Part of the problem with going to the Eastman Jewish Academy is that she had known all the boys there since kindergarten. The boys were more like brothers than boyfriends. She knew that she would never have a boyfriend among her fellow students.

Isar smirked. "Maybe you will meet a boyfriend at Bobby's party tonight."

Joshua looked surprised, "What party tonight?"

"Bobby Jenkins, who goes to Taft High School. His parents are out of town, and he has the house to himself. He invited me to come and bring some friends. Katy and Miriam are coming, and several other students. He promised me there would be a keg of beer." His voice moved to a stage whisper. "There will be some other things to make the evening enjoyable. I hope you are all coming."

Miriam touched Katy's arm. "We're going." Katy gave a bit of a guilty smile, knowing that her parents would not approve.

David said, "Sorry, I can't make it. My grandma's in from out of town and we are having a Shabbat dinner. It seems that my mom only lights candles and sets a Shabbat dinner when my grandma's in town. Hopefully my parents will not tell her I am gay. I don't think she could handle it. How could she tell the ladies in her mahjong group about her gay grandson?"

The others turned to Joshua. He answered in a soft voice, "You know I can't go. It is Friday night. My parents require me to be home for Sabbath dinner. My sister and I are not allowed to go out on Friday night - period, let alone to some party at a non-Jewish home."

"How would your parents know?" Isar replied. "As well as

beer and weed, there will be girls there. Not the uptight girls from this school, all nice and virginal." He gave a glance at Miriam and Katy. "Girls from the public school. Girls with some experience. Come with us."

"What will I tell my parents?"

"Tell your parents you are coming to my house to study for an exam. Tell them that we will have a Shabbat dinner, *kiddush* and everything at my home. They will never know the difference."

Joshua never lied to his parents. But he was also growing tired of their restrictive lifestyle. Why should he not join his classmates for a party on Friday night? He took out his phone and texted his mom. "Mom, not coming home for Shabbat dinner tonight. Going to Isar's to study. Will make *kiddush* there. Tell Dad sorry." He knew that his mom would be more understanding of his not coming home. To his dad, it was very important that he be home every Friday night. "The deed is done," he said.

When Isar and Joshua arrived at Bobby's home around 7 pm, the party was in full swing. They heard the music from the outside and smelled both beer and weed as soon as they entered the large, two-story house. Bobby lived in a fancy neighborhood about ten miles from their school. It was a neighborhood of professionals, businessmen, doctors, and lawyers. Like many of the adults in their neighborhood, Bobby's parents travelled a lot. Now they were on a week-long river cruise down the Danube. And Bobby planned to enjoy his parents' absence.

Joshua looked around the room and saw numerous kids he did not know, kids who went to the public high school, kids of various ethnicities and nationalities. He also saw a number of his classmates. Miriam and Katy were sitting on a couch in the center of the room. Miriam held a red plastic cup of beer. Several of the boys were already trying to flirt with Miriam, who had developed a well-practiced way of dismissing them. The boys were ignoring Katy. Isar handed Joshua a cup of beer and said, "Come on, my friend, time to find some girls."

Joshua was not particularly interested in meeting girls. Most of the girls were not Jewish, and his parents would never allow him to date them or even spend time with them. And most of the Jewish girls he had known since childhood, either from his school or from the synagogue. But he did not want to disappoint Isar, so he followed him from room to room. He admired Isar's self-confidence, his ability to talk to almost anyone. It was the Israeli personality. Joshua had always been more reserved. Perhaps it was because he grew up in the home of a rabbi, who was such a powerful presence in the community. To some extent, Joshua always felt inadequate next to his father.

The boys came into the family room where a baseball game was playing on the flat screen tv. Few of the young people were watching, but the television created background noise, making everyone speak a bit louder. Here the smell of the weed was stronger. Someone handed Isar a blunt and he inhaled deeply. He then handed it to Joshua. Joshua had grown up in a home where it was forbidden even to light a match on the Sabbath. He imagined what his father would think if he saw him smoking a joint on Friday night. His father would probably ground him for a month. Joshua took the blunt and inhaled deeply. The smoke filled his lungs. He had smoked weed at Isar's home, but never at a party. Joshua inhaled again. He found his mind relaxing, growing a bit more distant from all the activity around him. He wanted to simply sit on the couch and chill. How could Isar try to pick up girls when he was high? He took a deep breath and watched as Isar went to the keg and poured himself a second cup of beer.

Nicolas Velazzi was already bored. He came to the party because Bobby Jenkins was his best friend. He did not drink. His deeply religious Catholic parents would be horrified if he tried drugs. He did not dance. And he lacked the confidence to try to pick up girls. So, he wondered from room to room, trying to strike up a conversation with anybody who would speak to him. Most of the party goers were busy drinking beer and speaking loudly with one another, or smoking weed and feeling mellow under the influence of the cannabis. A few were watching sports on the large television. Nicolas wondered how long he ought to stay before he could leave to go home. He had called an Uber to get there and would call another when he had fulfilled his obligation to stay.

It was then that Nicolas wondered into the living room and saw Miriam and Katy. He did not recognize them. One was very pretty and seemed to gather the attention of one boy after another. She was able to expertly wave them off. The other sat next to her, looking alone in the midst of the crowd. Something about her deep brown eyes drew Nicolas to her. Her eyes seemed very kind and understanding.

Nicolas walked up to her. "Can I bring you a drink?"

Katy responded, "I don't drink. How about a coke?" Nicolas filled a glass with ice, poured a coke, and sat down next to Katy. This was the most forward he could remember being with a girl in a long time.

He showed her his cup. "I don't drink either. I guess we will be the two coke drinkers in this beer party. I don't think we have met. Do you go to Taft High School? I know some of the students there, but I do not remember seeing you before."

She put out her hand. "I'm Katy. I go to the Eastman Jewish Academy. It is a Jewish parochial school."

"I'm Nicolas. Some call me Nick but I prefer Nicolas. I guess we have something in common. I go to St. Anselm, a Catholic High School. That's why I do not know many of the students here. I did not even know there was a Jewish parochial high school. Your parents must be pretty religious."

"Not really," Katy answered. "My mom belongs to a synagogue but usually only goes on the Jewish High Holidays. They tell me that I should go there in order to get into a better college. I think the real reason they send me there is so that I will meet and date Jewish boys."

"You only date Jewish boys?"

"I really don't date anyone at all. My friend here, Miriam, she has been seeing a college student, but he is away at school now. I mostly hang out with friends."

Nicolas glanced across her to Miriam, then looked back at Katy. "My parents are different. They are very religious. My dad is a deacon at St. Anselm's Catholic Church. They make me go with them to mass each Sunday. Even confession at least once a month. But I am not sure what I believe. The school drives me a bit crazy with the religion classes."

Katy stared at him. "I have always wanted to ask a question to someone Catholic. Does your Church talk a lot about the Jews?"

"They talk about how Jesus was Jewish."

"Not Jews in Jesus's day. Jews today. Do you learn about them?"

Nicolas thought for a moment. "The Church is changing. I remember about five years ago; we were having an interfaith service on the Wednesday before Thanksgiving. Our Catholic Church, the Protestant churches, even a local synagogue were participating. The rabbi was supposed to deliver the homily."

"What's a homily?"

"A kind of a sermon. I remember it was a Rabbi Williams who was supposed to speak."

"He is my rabbi," said Katy.

"Anyway, we had this old priest who was head of our local parish, very old school. He said that he would not permit a rabbi to speak in the parish. He would give the homily himself. Rabbi

Williams attended, and our two younger priests apologized to him. They were embarrassed. The way our old priest acted you would have thought that Rabbi Williams killed Jesus. Anyway, that old priest is now retired, and things are changing in the Church."

The way our old priest acted you would have thought that Rabbi Williams was Judas Iscariot himself."

Katy interrupted, "Who was Judas Iscariot?"

Nicholas blinked in surprise, and then answered, "Judas Iscariot sold out the location of where Jesus and his disciples were staying - at the Garden of Gethsemane. You know, for thirty pieces of silver. And when they showed up with Roman soldiers, Judas kissed Jesus to identify him to the soldiers."

Katy gasped, "*The Judas kiss*! I've heard of that but didn't understand it."

Nicholas grinned, pleased at helping Katy learn something new about his religion. Katy smiled back and then blushed. Nicholas dropped his gaze and cleared his throat, "Anyway, that old priest is now retired, and things are changing in the Church."

Nicolas continued, "Last year, our school invited a rabbi to speak to our high school students. I remember him – black hat, black coat, with these strings hanging out from his shirt."

"*Tzitzit*."

"What?"

"They are called *tzitzit*, ritual fringes. Orthodox Jews wear them to remember all of God's commandments. It sounds like you are describing Rabbi Lebovic."

24

"That was his name. Most of us have Jewish friends. In fact, I went to a few bar mitzvahs when I was younger. But this was the first time I ever had a rabbi teach us about Judaism. I would love to learn more about it."

Katy responded, "I would love to learn more about your religion. I do not think the Eastman Jewish Academy has ever invited a Catholic priest to speak."

They were interrupted by Miriam, pointing to her phone. "My dad is calling. I think we need to start home."

Katy turned to Nicolas. "My friend needs to go, and she is my ride. It was nice meeting you, Nicolas."

"Nice meeting you, Katy. Tell me, would you like to hang out one day this week?"

"I told you my parents don't allow me to date non-Jews."

"My parents don't allow me to date non-Catholics. This is not a date. Just hanging out."

Katy took his phone and punched in her number. "Text me." And the two girls left.

As they were walking to the door, Miriam said, "Sorry to pull you away from that boy. But the guys here were not leaving me alone. My dad did not call me, I called him. Thank God Kevin is coming home next weekend. Although I will have to sneak out to see him."

Katy laughed, "Just tell your dad you are going to my house." They stood outside until they saw Barry Pollack pull up in his blue Mercedes.

Joshua walked up to Isar, who was arguing loudly with some other boys about baseball. "Isar, I think I am ready to go home."

"Come on. The party's beginning to get fun. Let me at least have another beer."

"How many is that Isar, four or five?"

"Five, maybe six. Who is counting?" Isar slurred.

"Isar. You're drunk. You are in no condition to drive."

"I am fine. After the beer, I will drive you home."

Joshua knew that he could not get into a car with his friend, and he should not let his friend drive. "Isar, give me your car keys."

"Stop being a wuss," Isar shouted. He walked to the keg and poured another beer. He was stumbling as he walked.

Joshua knew that there was no choice. He would have to call his parents. He knew that his dad did not like answering the phone on the Jewish Sabbath. But he would pick up if the call was from him. Joshua had a sinking feeling in his stomach. His dad would be furious. He phoned his dad's cell phone.

"Dad, I'm sorry. I know it is Shabbat. ... I am not at Isar's. ... We went to a party, this kid named Bobby. I am sorry. But I need you. I need you to come pick me up. Maybe you can also get Isar to give up the car keys." Joshua gave his dad the address and went to wait outside. Fifteen minutes later, Rabbi Williams drove up.

"I am sorry, Dad."

"I have always told you that you can call me anytime, even

on Shabbat. I would rather you call me than you get into a car with a friend who is drunk. We will talk later."

Joshua started to get into the car, but his dad signaled for him to follow. He walked into Bobby's home. When the tall rabbi wearing a black yarmulke walked into the party, the noise died down. What was he doing there? Rabbi Williams walked straight up to Isar, who was still arguing with some other kids.

"Isar, give me your car keys. I am driving you home."

"I am fine, Rabbi. Take your son home. I will go later."

Rabbi Williams moved closer to him. "Isar, I am not telling you again. Give me your car keys. I am driving you home."

"How am I supposed to get my car home?"

"You will pick it up tomorrow when you are sober. Give me your car keys now."

"No! I am fine."

The Rabbi turned to his son. "Dial 911. Let's get the police here."

"Wait." Isar handed the rabbi his keys. His hand was shaking. At that moment, Nicolas, who had been listening to this, walked over to the rabbi.

"Sir, I have not had anything to drink. I don't drink. Give me the keys and I will drive him home in his car. I know him and I don't live far from his house. I can drive him to his house and walk home." Nicolas had met Isar only once at Bobby's house, but he remembered where he lived.

"You have had nothing to drink?"

"I swear in Jesus's name," he said as he crossed himself.

The Rabbi had to smile. By now everybody was watching. The room had grown silent. He handed Nicolas the keys and said to Isar, "He will drive you home – now. I will wait until you are both in the car." Then he scanned the room. "Kids, the party is over. Time for you all to go home."

The Rabbi waited until kids began walking out. He then walked with Joshua back to the car. Joshua started to talk but the Rabbi stopped him. "We will talk tomorrow. After synagogue. I want you in synagogue with me tomorrow morning. Be dressed by eight." They drove home in silence.

2. FIRST CLASS
THE RABBI AND THE PROSTITUTE

I was surprisingly nervous as I waited for the students to file in. It was strange feeling more nervous before speaking to a small group of high school seniors than giving a sermon to a thousand people on Yom Kippur. Perhaps it was the feeling that with this class, I was challenging the practices of the entire liberal Jewish community.

The Jews I served no longer believed or practiced Orthodox Judaism. Their values came not from the Torah but from the general ethos of liberal America. Premarital sex was not only acceptable but expected. I remember a movie about a man entering middle age and still a virgin. His friends try to help him gain sexual experience. It was very enjoyable but also very troubling. The underlying premise was that anyone who reaches the age of forty without sexual experience is abnormal. In addition, over the last couple of decades homosexuality had become acceptable. In truth, I had no problem with either pre-martial or gay sexual activity. When I performed a wedding, I did not expect the couples sitting before me to wait until marriage before they consummated the act. Even as a rabbi, I am a product of the prevalent liberal American culture.

What bothered me as I prepared the class was something deeper. Sex was no longer holy. In fact, for young people, sex had become recreational, something one did for fun. Like recreational drugs, recreational sex had become the norm. It was no different from bowling or listening to music, an activity with no consequences beyond the pleasure of the moment. In fact, many young people considered such activities as oral sex not to be sex at all. It was simply something someone did, mostly young girls to young boys, to win favor. Sex had become casual. It seems to me as a result, there has been an explosion of teen pregnancies, abortions, and even sexually transmitted diseases among young people.

I was teaching this class to try to slow down a cultural tidal wave that was overwhelming liberal America. My goal was to convince a small group of teenage students in one school in America that sex is something holy, to be reserved for the right person in the right context. It was an idea that defied all the cultural norms these young people were learning.

My students gathered. There were twenty-four students in the senior class, but five of them were not allowed to take the class by their parents. The other nineteen all showed up. My son sat in the back facing the window, looking embarrassed. I know he was unhappy that his friend Isar was not in the class. But he looked more uncomfortable than usual. Maybe he was still embarrassed by the events of last Friday night and the discussion after synagogue Saturday afternoon. More likely, he did not want to hear his father talk about such topics as masturbation and orgasms. In a sense, I did not blame him.

I remember my own father's awkward attempt to tell me about what to expect when I married - what I should expect on my wedding night. He stood behind his workbench in his shed, where he repaired and refinished furniture for friends, families, and strangers as a hobby. "It will be messy," he nodded. "But if you are patient, she will present you with a child. And by that, God is good." That was the extent of my marital advice from my father. I looked again at my son, hunching over his desk in the hope that he might become invisible. I prayed I would do a better job explaining sexual matters to my son.

Barry Pollack's daughter Miriam came in together with the young lady she spent all her time with – what was her name? – Katy. The girls were giggling. I was amazed how pretty Miriam had become since her bat mitzvah. No wonder her father was worried about guys. I wondered if she was still seeing her college friend Kevin. Another of my son's friends, David, came in and sat next to my son. Joshua told me that he was gay, as far as I knew, the only gay student in the class. Or at least, the only one who had come out of the closet so far.

The class settled down and I asked each student to tell me his or her name. I knew most of them, but I did not want to embarrass anyone, so I went around the room. When it was Joshua's turn, he said, "Dad, are you really asking me for my name?"

"Yes, maybe there are students who do not know you."

"Dad, we have been together since kindergarten. They all know me."

I saw my father, so focused on his refinishing hobby, more familiar with the way to weave cane into a chair seat than who my friends were in junior high. I let Joshua's dismissal pass.

After the students had introduced themselves, I began. "Let me give you the rules of this class. We are going to speak honestly about numerous topics. We will use the real anatomical terms – penis, vagina, clitoris." A few students giggled, but I raised my hand to quiet them. "I expect us to approach this without laughing. No topic is off-limits."

Katy raised her hand, "Rabbi, what's a clitoris?"

Gary Brown gave her a sharp look. Gary was always the smart aleck. "Come on Katy, don't you know? That's how a woman feels sexual pleasure."

I thought that these students had learned the basics in middle school health. But obviously there was a lot of learning to do. Katy was probably not the only one who did not know. "The clitoris is a tiny organ above the vagina on a woman. It allows a woman to feel sexual pleasure. In some places, particularly in Africa, they practice female genital mutilation. They remove the clitoris so women will not feel pleasure in sex. Most of the world considers it a violation of human rights."

Gary spoke out again. "You mean female circumcision."

I grew impatient. "No! It is not female circumcision. Circumcision removes a piece of skin covering the penis. It is a central ritual in Judaism. Removing it often increases sexual pleasure. Genital mutilation removes an entire organ."

Gary spoke up again. "Some people consider removing the clitoris on a young woman as a religious act, just like you consider removing the foreskin on an eight-day old baby a religious act. Who are we to judge one religion better than another?"

This discussion was going in a direction that I did not wish to go. "Gary, that discussion will have to wait for another time. I want to get back on track. We are going to study a passage today from the Talmud. It actually is a passage encouraging the wearing of *tzitzit*."

Shmuel shouted out. "You mean like these?" as he held up one of the four fringes he wore hanging out of his shirt. I still knew Shmuel by his given name Steven. His parents were members of my congregation, but almost completely non-religious. His mother was on my synagogue board. Shmuel's parents were taken aback when their son started wearing a yarmulke and ritual fringes all the time, when he started using his Hebrew name, when he insisted on eating only kosher, and spending Friday night and Saturday with Rabbi Lebovic. The only difference from strict Orthodoxy was that Shmuel had a blue thread in his four fringes. The Bible requires a thread of blue, but mainstream Orthodoxy had ceased using it years ago. Now a small group of Hasidic Jews in Israel were reintroducing the blue thread.

"Yes, like those," I said. "I believe the class knows what *tzitzit* are. This story in the Talmud explains why we should wear them."

"What does that have to do with sex?" said Gary.

"Everything. Let's begin the story."

I passed out copies of the Talmudic passage in English. I could have included the Hebrew and have them study it in the original; most of their Hebrew was adequate. But I wanted to focus on the story itself. I asked for a volunteer to read and Lewis, an African American student whose parents had converted to Judaism years ago, raised his hand. I nodded. He stood and began to read:

The Rabbi and the Prostitute

(Talmud – *Menachot* 44a)

It is taught in a *Baraita* [Rabbinic source], that Rabbi Natan says: There is no *mitzvah*, however minor, that is written in the Torah, for which there is no reward given in this world; and in the World-to-Come I do not know how much reward is given.

Go and learn from the following incident concerning the *mitzvah* of *tzitzit* [ritual fringes] incident involving a certain man who was diligent about the *mitzvah* of *tzitzit*. This man heard that there was a prostitute in one of the cities overseas who took four hundred gold coins as her payment. He sent her four hundred gold coins and fixed a time to meet with her. When his time came, he came and sat at the entrance to her house.

The maidservant of that prostitute entered and said to her: That man who sent you four hundred gold coins came and sat at the entrance. She said: Let him enter. He entered. She arranged seven beds for him, six of silver and one of gold. Between each and every one of them there was a ladder made of silver, and the top bed was had a ladder that was made of gold.

She went up and sat naked on the top bed, and he too went up in order to sit naked facing her. In the meantime, his four *tzitzit* came and slapped him on his face. He dropped down and sat himself on the ground, and she also dropped down and sat on the ground. She said to him: I take an oath by the Roman Capitol that I will not allow you to go until you tell me what defect you saw in me.

He said to her: I take an oath by the Temple service that I never saw a woman as beautiful as you. But there is one *mitzvah* that the Lord, our God, commanded us, and its name is *tzitzit*, and in the passage where it is commanded, it is written twice: "I am the Lord your God" (Numbers 15:41). The doubling of this phrase indicates: I am the one who will punish those who transgress My *mitzvot*, and I am the one who will reward those who fulfill them. Now, said the man, the four sets of *tzitzit* appeared to me as if they were four witnesses who will testify against me.

She said to him: I will not allow you to go until you tell me: What is your name, and what is the name of your city, and what is the name of your teacher, and what is the name of the study hall in which you studied Torah? He wrote the information and placed it in her hand.

She arose and divided all of her property, giving one-third to the government, one-third to the poor, and she took one-third with her in her possession, in addition to those beds of gold and silver.

She came to the study hall of Rabbi Ḥiyya and said to him: My teacher, have your students instruct me and have them make me a convert. Rabbi Ḥiyya said to her: My daughter, perhaps you set your sights on one of the students and that is why you want to convert? She took the note the student had given her from her hand and gave it to Rabbi Ḥiyya. He [converted her and] said to her: Go take possession of your purchase.

Those beds that she had arranged for him in a prohibited fashion, she now arranged for him in a permitted fashion. This is the reward given to him in this world, and with regard to the World-to-Come, I do not know how much reward he will be given.

After Lewis read the story, Shmuel was the first to speak out. "That story could not be true. No rabbi would convert a prostitute, particularly to marry a rabbi that she was doing business with. I am going ask Rabbi Lebovic if that story is really in the Talmud."

"Go ahead. In those days, conversion was much simpler than today. People converted for marriage." I then turned to the class. "What is the point of the story?"

Shmuel answered, "That we should wear *tzitzit*."

"That is true. But there is another message. At the beginning of the story, a man and woman were about to have sex on seven mattresses, six of silver and one of gold. At the end of the story that same man and woman did have sex on seven mattresses, six of silver and one of gold. It was the same physical act. What is the difference?"

Miriam answered, "In the end, they were married."

"True," I said. "But look a little deeper. In the beginning, why were they having sex? What did the man want and what did the woman want?"

My son opened his mouth. "The man wanted the pleasure of sex with a beautiful woman. Obviously, he could afford it. And the woman wanted the money."

"Correct. In the beginning they only saw themselves and

their needs. And what about the end?"

Again, Joshua answered, "In the end, they saw each other."

"Good. Jewish tradition says that sex is not legitimate when people only see themselves and their own needs. It becomes legitimate only when they see each other. I am going to give you a basic idea – *kedusha*. It means holiness.

"Let me give you a definition of holiness. Holiness is rising above the animal within us. Let's apply that to sex. How do animals have sex?"

Lewis spoke out. "Animals only have sex when the female is in heat."

"Good," I said. "That is a fundamental teaching. Animals only have sex when there is potential to lead to pregnancy. Humans can have sex even without pregnancy. That will be a major issue as we continue in this class. Why did God allow us humans to be sexually active even when there is no chance of pregnancy? Save that for a future class. What is another sexual difference between animals and people?"

The class pondered my question. Finally, I spoke. "Most animals have sex by the male mounting the female. It is face to back. Most of the time, humans have sex face-to-face. They see each other's faces. In fact, the Midrash teaches, *All living creatures mate face to back except two who mate back-to-back, the dog and the camel. And three mate face to face because God's presence dwells between them, the man, the snake, and the fish.* I doubt the rabbis were accurate about their zoology. But perhaps there is some deep truth about the fact that humans mate face-to-face because God dwells between them. In Judaism, sex should take place when people see each other."

I could see that David was ready to jump out of his chair. "Is that why Judaism hates gays? Because gays do not have sex face to face."

Gary answered back to him, "Why don't you tell us how gays have sex?"

"Enough," I had to smile at Gary's comeback. "First, Judaism does not hate gays. The whole issue of gays and sex will have to wait for a future class. Our time is up. Think about the story of the rabbi and the prostitute, and what it means to rise above the animal. Class dismissed."

I noticed my son was the first out the door.

3. THE FAKE ID

After school on Monday, Isar and Joshua drove to the mall. At the food court, Isar ordered a cheeseburger while Joshua ordered a fish filet. He could still not bring himself to defy his parents by eating non-kosher meat out of the house. They shared a large fries and found a table.

Joshua asked his friend, "What happened to you Friday night? Did your parents find out that you were so drunk, that someone had to drive you home?"

Isar laughed. "By the time I got home, my parents were asleep. They had to get up early to go to work Saturday. I woke up with a bad hangover, but my parents never knew. Thank God they work so many hours, they barely know what I do."

Joshua looked at his friend. "Your dad is so religious that he does not think my dad is a real rabbi. Yet he goes to work every Saturday instead of going to synagogue. I don't understand."

Isar became serious. "My dad goes to work every day, seven days a week. You know that he owns a jewelry shop booth at the flea market. The owners of the flea market require their shop owners to be there 365 days a year. They advertise that they are open every day of the year, even Christmas. The Christian owners complain, but the owner told them, if you want to keep your business, open your store on Christmas. And the place is packed Christmas day; many of the Jews shop on that day."

Isar continued, "Did you know that when my dad first opened the shop, he and some of the other Israelis who run shops there tried to close on Yom Kippur. They gave the owner of the flea market a petition saying that it was the holiest day of the year, they needed to close. The owner laughed at them. *If the Christians can open on Christmas, then you Jews can open on Yom Kippur.* The first year my dad closed anyway. He received a letter of reprimand and a thousand dollar fine. The owner said it was in his contract. So, for several years, my dad went in even on Yom Kippur. Now he has a non-Jewish woman he trusts, who goes in and covers the shop on the holiest days of the year. My dad is not happy with the situation, but he earns a good living."

"I cannot imagine your dad working on Yom Kippur."

"When you have to earn a living, sometimes there is no choice. But what about you? Did your parents ground you?"

Joshua sat back. "I was surprised. I went to synagogue with my dad and sister, and when we got home, my mom had laid out a whole Shabbat lunch. Tuna, egg salad, cheese, bagels. My dad started to talk. He told me that he was glad I called him rather than drive home with you. But then he said that I broke the rules of the house, and he needs to ground me."

"Your dad really grounded you for going to a party on Friday night?"

"Let me finish. My mom interrupted my dad. She told my dad." Joshua held up his hand and used his voice to mimic his mother, "*Hold on. Our son is seventeen years old. He is at an age where he can decide whether to go out with his friends. I know you want him home Friday night for Shabbat dinner. So do I. But I think at this age it has to be his choice. I can think of no better way to make a kid hate religion than to force it down their throat. Let him decide.*

"Isar, my mouth fell open. My mom saying I did not need to be home for Shabbat dinner. My dad simply said okay. I told my parents, *Don't worry, I will usually be home. But sometimes I need to go out with my friends.* Then my dad repeated," Joshua deepened his voice with a fake pompous impression of his father, "*I want you to feel free to call me anytime, even Friday night, if you are stranded and need a way to get home.* I was not grounded. I am still surprised by my parents' attitude. My sister Shira immediately asked, *what about me? Can I go out with friends on Friday night?* My dad told her, *you're only fourteen. Let's talk when you are seventeen.* That was the whole conversation."

"Listen, there are other parties. We'll go again."

"Not if you get drunk." Just then they spotted a classmate, Heather Hall, walking towards them carrying some kind of coffee drink. She had obviously changed out of her school uniform into shorts, a tank top that revealed her trim midriff, and a pair of sandals. Heather dressed in a way that ignored all of Rabbi Lebovic lectures about *tznius* – modesty. She liked to show off her body, and the boys in the class took notice. Isar waved her over to join them.

"Heather, how was the rabbi's sex class?"

"Not bad. Except, sorry to say this Joshua, he came across as sexist."

"Sexist?" Joshua proclaimed. He knew his father had fought in the synagogue to call women to the Torah and count them in the *minyan*. His father had his faults, but sexism was not one of them.

"Yeah, he told this crazy story which he claimed was from the Talmud. It was about a rabbi and a prostitute. The story really bothered me. Here was a successful businesswoman, earning such a good living she could afford six mattresses of silver and one of gold. Then she meets this rabbi. He won't have sex with her unless she converts and marries him. So, the poor woman closes down her business, gives much of her wealth away, converts, and becomes the rabbi's wife. What is she going to do now for a living? Bake kugels? In my mind, she should have kept her business and told the rabbi where to go."

Joshua replied, "Heather, the whole point of the story was to compare illegitimate and legitimate sex. Sex between a rabbi and a prostitute is illegitimate; between two married people is legitimate."

"I know. The rabbi is going to try to tell us that sex is only legitimate within a marriage. Does he want people to marry at eighteen? I think that all rabbis, all priests, all ministers, and imams need to get a life. Lots of people have sex outside marriage, and it is absolutely legitimate." The look on Heather's face said that she was one of those *lots of people.* Joshua thought that maybe the word circulating through the school about Heather was true. Then he heard Isar's voice.

"Rabbis and prostitutes. This class sounds more interesting than I thought it would be. Study hall is boring. I am going to ask my dad again to give me permission to take the class."

Two weeks later, Isar had joined the other seniors in the rabbi's sex class.

Joshua, Isar, and Heather never saw Katy at the mall. She was sitting across the food court next to the Starbucks, talking to Nicolas, the young man she met at the party. Katy had told Nicolas that she was not allowed to date non-Jews. Nicolas told Katy that he could not date non-Catholics. But this was not a date, they just met up at the mall to talk. Each had ordered a frappuccino and were already immersed in a heavy discussion about religion.

Katy told Nicolas, "You know in my religion, rabbis are expected to be married. Some say they are required to marry. We learned in the Talmud that Ben Azai said, anyone who does not marry and have children, it is as if he spilled blood. Of course, Ben Azai never married. He told his students he was married to the Torah." Katy was amazed that she could still quote this passage from the Talmud that she had learned from Rabbi Lebovic.

"Personally, I think it is a good thing for religious leaders to be married. So tell me, why can't nuns or priests marry?"

"I suppose it is the same answer. Your rabbi said he was married to the Torah. Nuns say they are married to Jesus. I guess the whole thing goes back to St. Paul, who never married. Neither did Jesus nor most of the apostles. Paul said that it is best that people be like him – unmarried. But if they cannot control themselves, let them marry. I remember the quote from my religion class. *Better to marry than to burn.*"

Katy looked at him, "You mean they burnt people who had sex outside of marriage?"

Nicolas answered, "I think he means that it is better to marry than to burn with passion. In the Church, marriage is a compromise. The ideal is celibacy, taking a vow like a priest. That way the priest can truly serve his parish without worrying about his family or his kids. How does your rabbi serve a big congregation while worrying about his wife and kids at home?"

"I don't know. He manages. His son Joshua is in my class. You remember him from the party last Friday night."

Nicolas reacted, "He is the rabbi who came into the party and sent everyone home. I drove that Israeli kid, what's his name – Isar. He was wasted."

"We are all seniors together. Isar, the rabbi's son Joshua, me, my best friend Miriam. Her father is president of the synagogue." Katy paused for a second. "Nicolas, can I ask you a rough question? If priests have to take a vow of celibacy, if they have to follow Paul and not have sex, if that makes them holy, then why are there so many scandals involving priests and young boys? I hope you are not mad at me for asking."

"Katy, you can ask me anything. The scandals were horrible. Many people quit the Church. Luckily it never hit my parish, St. Anselm. I don't know why. But I have a theory." He lowered his voice, "I think there are men who have sexual perversions, who are attracted to boys. Many learn to control it, to avoid acting on it. I think some men join the priesthood because they think the vow of celibacy will help them control the urges. But once they get into a parish, surrounded by choir boys, they find the urge very difficult to control."

"I understand. If I can quote another rabbi, Ben Zoma, he said, *Who is strong? Whoever can control their urges.*"

"Is that rabbi still around?"

Katy laughed, "He died almost 2000 years ago. He was a rabbi in the Talmud. But there are rabbis today who have the same problem as priests. I know of one rabbi who is in jail because he could not control his urges with young boys. The rest of his life he will be labeled a sex offender. He certainly will never work as a rabbi again. And he will never be allowed to work around children."

"I guess both of our religions teach self-control when it comes to sex. Mine says that self-control comes only from absolute celibacy. Yours at least allows rabbis to marry."

"True, but I imagine rabbis cheat on their spouses as much as anyone else. My parents had a horrible marriage. They were constantly fighting. They are now happily divorced. I am not sure that I believe in marriage."

"I am sorry to hear that." Nicolas leaned over close to Katy and took her hand. Then, before he realized what he was doing, he gave her a kiss. She held the kiss for a moment before pulling away. Then Nicolas said, "Katy Roberts. I would like to see you again."

"How about Friday after school? My parents don't need to know."

"Friday it is." He leaned over and kissed her again. She held it even longer. As she walked away, she thought of her parents. Even after the divorce, they were still bickering. There was only one thing they agreed with: she should only date Jews. And here she was, kissing a boy from a religious Catholic home in the food court of the mall. Katy smiled.

David Eisenberg was extremely nervous as he walked to the apartment entrance. He felt like a sheltered white boy venturing into unknown and dangerous territory. Kevin's college roommate Ted had given him this address. He did not realize that it was in the heart of the inner-city blight.

When he called, the gruff sounding man had told to come alone and bring $200 in cash. Everything about the apartment building seemed dilapidated, from the broken handrail to the graffiti on the walls. He hoped that his car, parked directly outside, would be ok when he returned. David walked to the third story and knocked on the door.

"*Quien esta?*" shouted a voice.

"This is David. You said I could come over now."

"*Estas solo?* Are you alone?"

"Yes.

A big Hispanic man with a large mustache and multiple tattoos across his shoulders and arms opened the door. He did not give his name. "Show me your driver's license."

David pulled out the license and the man looked at the picture.

"You look too young in this picture. Put on these glasses and put on a shirt and tie. It will make you look older."

David was surprised that the man had a shirt and tie to loan him right in the apartment. David changed and put on the glasses. He thought they made him look dorky. But Ted said the man knew what he was doing.

"Do you have *dinero*, the money?"

David handed him $200 in cash; two weeks' work at the local pizza parlor. The man carefully counted the money, then snapped a picture and went to work on a machine. A half hour later he showed David his handiwork. It was a perfect driver's license, showing David to be twenty-one years old this last February. "I always put the real birthday but add a few years. Sometimes when you hand them a fake ID, they ask your birthday. *Se bien?* Does it look good?"

"Perfect," said David.

"Remember, I am the best in the business. Recommend your

friends to me." He opened the door and let David out into the stairwell. David was relieved to see his car intact, and quickly drove back to the suburbs. He would put this fake ID to good use when Ted came into town in a few weeks.

4. SECOND CLASS
THE EVIL INCLINATION

My students entered the room joking and gossiping, in a good mood. We were up to twenty students now that Joshua's friend Isar was in the class. The two boys sat next to each other towards the back. My son seemed much happier, less resistant to everything, with his friend there. I hoped that Isar would not start making comments he had heard from his father, that I am not a real rabbi and my Judaism is not real Judaism.

It took me a moment to settle them down and get quiet. "In the previous class, we came up with a definition of *kedushah* – holiness. Holiness is what separates us from animals. When animals have sex, it is a biological act. The idea is for humans to make it into more than a biological act. How do we do that? I gave you a hint last class."

I paused but nobody spoke up. "Ok, most of the time animals have sex with both animals facing in the same direction. The male mounts the female. Humans have sex, at least most the time, face to face. What is the importance of that?"

Miriam Pollack answered. "They can see each other."

"Right, Miriam, and why is that important?" I paused for a moment to let them consider the question. Then I continued, "Anybody know the Biblical word for sexual intercourse? You learned it in Bible class. What does it say when Adam and Eve had their first sexual encounter?"

Miriam continued, "Adam knew his wife."

"Correct. You need to know your sexual partner; you need to see your sexual partner. You need to know their needs. And this points to the problem in the story we read last week, the story of the rabbi and the prostitute. At the beginning, they did not know each other. They were not looking at each other. Each was looking at themselves. He was thinking about his pleasure. She was thinking about her money. Only in the end, after they married, did they truly know each other."

Gary Brown's hand immediately shot up, but he did not even wait for me to call on him. "Rabbi, are you saying that only married couples know each other well enough to have sex? That sex belongs only in marriage?"

"I did not say that. We will talk about sex outside of marriage, whether it is right or wrong. But for right now I am talking about people seeing each other, knowing each other."

Gary continued, "Good, because I know plenty of married people that don't know each other."

Katy spoke out, "Before my parents got divorced, they

barely knew each other. They could not stand each other. In fact, I think they stopped having sex long before their divorce."

"That is sad. As a rabbi, that is what I try to prevent. Let us continue. We are going to read two Biblical verses. One speaks of the creation of animals, and one speaks of the creation of humans." I passed out a paper with the two verses in Hebrew and English.

וַיִּיצֶר יְהֹוָה אֱלֹהִים אֶת־הָאָדָם עָפָר מִן־הָאֲדָמָה וַיִּפַּח
בְּאַפָּיו נִשְׁמַת חַיִּים וַיְהִי הָאָדָם לְנֶפֶשׁ חַיָּה:

"And the Lord God formed man of the dust of the ground and breathed into his nostrils the breath of life; and man became a living soul." (Genesis 2:7)

וַיִּצֶר יְהֹוָה אֱלֹהִים מִן־הָאֲדָמָה כָּל־חַיַּת הַשָּׂדֶה וְאֵת כָּל־
עוֹף הַשָּׁמַיִם וַיָּבֵא אֶל־הָאָדָם לִרְאוֹת מַה־יִּקְרָא־לוֹ וְכֹל אֲשֶׁר
יִקְרָא־לוֹ הָאָדָם נֶפֶשׁ חַיָּה הוּא שְׁמוֹ:

"And out of the ground the Lord God formed every beast of the field, and every bird of the air; and brought them to Adam to see what he would call them; and whatever Adam called every living creature, that was its name." (Genesis 2:19)

I had them read the two verses, first in Hebrew and then in English. We noted that the creation of humanity came first, then the creation of the animals.

"Good, now what Hebrew verb does the Torah use when it says *formed*? *Vayitzer*, from a root *yetzer* which means formed. The verb means to make something out of pre-existent matter, like clay. God formed them.

"Now look carefully. Can you see any difference in the Hebrew of the word *formed* when God made the man and when God made the animals?" The students stared at the Hebrew for a moment. Then, my son spoke. Good, at least he wasn't asleep.

"The word *vayitzer* is spelled differently in each case. The word has two *yuds* when God makes the man, but only one *yud* when God makes the animals."

The letter *yud* is the smallest Hebrew letter. I then asked, "What would account for the double use of the letter for the man and the single use for animals? This simple Hebrew fact leads to one of the most profound teachings in Jewish tradition. Anybody know why the word is spelled differently for humans and for animals?"

Gary Brown spoke up. "Probably some scribe in ancient times made a mistake."

I responded. "Possibly. But we can learn from such mistakes. Let me give you an answer, an answer that will be at the center of what we are learning in this class. The Hebrew word *yetzer* has a double meaning. It means *to form*. But it also means *appetite* or *inclination*.

"Why is there only one *yud* for animals? Because animals have only one inclination. They follow their appetites. We do not expect animals to make choices. They do what God created them to do. Tell me, if you owned a henhouse and a fox comes in at night and kills your hen, is that fox a sinner?"

The class seemed to all answer at once. "No."

"Of course not. Animals follow their instincts. They have one inclination. But humans have two *yud*s because we have two inclinations. The Rabbis gave those two inclinations names. We have a good inclination which the rabbis called the *yetzer hatov*. And we have the evil inclination which the rabbis called the *yetzer hara*."

Katy spoke out. "We learned about that in Rabbi Lebovic's class. He said we have a *yetzer hara* which is always trying to overwhelm us. He says we need to control our *yetzer*. I remember the quote from Ben Zoma, *Who is strong? Whoever controls their yetzer.* In fact, Rabbi Lebovic said that the sexual drive is the *yetzer hara*, the evil inclination. He told us how in his community they control it by marrying young. Girls often marry at seventeen or eighteen, and boys not much older."

"Rabbi Lebovic is correct. The rabbis did identify the sexual drive with the evil inclination. But I think that eighteen is too young to be married. There must be another way to control it. But before we get to that, tell me, is the evil inclination a bad thing. Should we try to remove it altogether?"

Shmuel responded, "That would probably make this a better world."

"The Rabbis of the Talmud taught that one day they captured the *yetzer hara*, the evil inclination, and put it in a barrel. They thought the world would become a better place. But they looked into the world and saw that everything had come to a halt. No one went to work, no one tried to have children, in fact according to the Talmud, no chicken laid an egg. They realized they had to release the *yetzer hara*. The world needs it."

I continued, "Why is that story in the Talmud?"

Again Miriam spoke. "We need our appetites. Without it we would not accomplish anything. We even need our sexual appetite." She giggled for a moment and then gained control. "Yes we need to control it, but without it no one would marry or have children."

"Good," I replied. Have any of you ever studied Sigmund Freud?"

This time Heather Hall answered. "He was the founder of psychoanalysis. My parents speak about him. But I thought he was a Jewish atheist."

I looked at her, the first time she had spoken in class. I knew with her strident feminist views, she probably had little use for Freud. "He was an atheist. Yet some of his teachings are very Jewish. He taught that our mind is made up of the id, the ego, and the superego. The id is all those hidden drives, in particular the drive for sex and the drive for violence. In so many ways the id resembles the evil inclination. Freud echoed the ancient rabbi Ben Zoma when he said we need to control the id, that this makes for a psychologically healthy individual."

I continued, "On the other hand the superego is the voice of your parents, your community, civilization, trying to get you to do the right thing. It is the *yetzer hatov*, the good inclination, telling us to do the right thing even when we do not want to. One of Freud's greatest books was called *Civilization and its Discontents*. Civilization is the good inclination, telling us what to do, but we do not want to listen. That is the discontent. The ego is the part of us which makes choices, decides between the good and the bad. And that is the key idea in Judaism. We can choose. Animals follow their appetites. Humans can decide whether or not to follow their appetites. These choices take place every day of your lives. You must decide what to do this afternoon. The *yetzer hatov*, good inclination, Freud's superego, says to study for the exam. The *yetzer hara*, evil inclination, Freud's id says to hang out with your friends. And your ego must make a choice."

I continued, "If this fight between the good and the evil inclination is important when you are studying for exams, how much more so when it comes to sexual behavior. Do you know which famous Biblical character was put to the test sexually?"

Shmuel answered, "King David?"

"Correct, King David. According to the Midrash, David asked God to put him to the test. God said he would, and even told him he would test his sexual self-control. David, this great king, bragged that he would pass such a test. That evening he saw Bathsheba bathing on a roof. Bathsheba was a married lady, but it did not matter. King David wanted her. He took her into his bed chamber, slept with her, then actually arranged to have her husband

Uriel killed in battle. David, as great as he was, committed both adultery and murder."

"Wait a second," Gary argued. "Didn't David and Bathsheba give birth to Solomon, who became a great king and built the Temple."

"Yes, but only after their first child died. The Bible says that this was punishment for David's sin."

Gary continued, "If a man as great as David could not control his inclination, how are we, mere high school students supposed to control it?" The class broke out in laughter, and even I smiled.

I decided to answer with a Talmudic story. "Once the great sage Abaye saw a young man and woman walking together through the field. In those days it was considered improper for a single man and woman to walk together. Abaye decided he would be a chaperone, walking behind them and making sure nothing unseemly happened. The two young people walked together for a distance, then went their separate ways. Abaye became extremely upset, went to see his teacher and banged his head against the wall. He told his teacher, had I been with that woman I would have been unable to control myself. His teacher answered, don't you know, the greater the man, the greater the inclination. Then Abaye felt better.

"Sometimes, particularly among accomplished men, the sexual drive is very great. That is why you hear of successful politicians, businessmen, celebrities, even television evangelists, even rabbis from some of the top pulpits in the country, who could not control their sexual drive. Freud would say that it was that very sexual drive, their id, which was channeled into their professional success. But the key idea for this class is that animals simply follow their inner drives. We humans can learn to control those drives. That is what makes us different from the animal world."

Gary spoke out again. "Rabbi I hate to disagree with you. There is no difference between humans and animals. We learned that in biology. We all come from the same ancestors, share the same genetic code. Humans are fancy animals. But scientists tell us we are just animals, maybe with a more complex brain but animals none the less."

Gary had thrown down the gauntlet, the same one thrown down by atheists such as Richard Dawkins and the late Christopher Hitchens at religious people such as myself. How can we say that humans are special, that humans are created in the image of God, when science says humans are not special? I knew that I would have to answer that question, sooner rather than later. But there was no time today. The bell rang and the class was dismissed.

5. MEMES AND EVOLUTION

Miriam sat on her bed, her iPad resting on her knees. The house was warm so she was wearing only a tee shirt. Everybody she knew seemed busy that afternoon. Her friend Katy was out with that boy she met a few weeks ago at the party. Even her younger brother Eddie was out with friends. Miriam decided to Facetime Kevin. He was usually in class or in the library at State College, but maybe she would be lucky. He answered immediately.

"Hey."

"Hey. Kevin, what are you doing?"

"Just in my dorm studying."

"I finished my homework."

"Are you at home? I thought you would be out with your friends after school. Where is Katy?"

"Everyone is busy. Even Katy. She has been seeing some guy she met at a party. Every day after school. She claims they are not dating, but they are sure spending time together."

"Katy with a guy. That is surprising. I wish I could be with you."

"You still coming next weekend?"

"The college is closed for three days. Veterans Day weekend. I really want to see you."

"Are you driving down alone?"

"No, my roommate Ted is driving with me. He lives too far away so he will stay at my parents' house for a few days."

"Is it strange, being roommate to a guy who's gay?"

"Not at all, I am as straight as they come. He has an excellent gay-dar, knowing who is straight and who is gay. He discusses guys he meets on campus with me. Asks me if they are cute."

"And do you discuss girls you meet on campus with him?"

"Miriam, I only have eyes for you. I don't even notice other girls."

"Bullshit. All guys notice other girls." She was a bit worried. She loved Kevin, but he had been pushing her to go all the way. She wasn't ready. Maybe on this trip she would allow him. But where? He was not allowed in her parents' home. His parents were fairly strict. Besides, Ted would be hanging around.

"Will Ted be with us when we're together?"

"I know he has some plans. You know that fellow David in your class. The one that came out of the closet last summer. He is planning to take David to this new gay bar that opened downtown."

She was surprised. "How can he take David? He's only seventeen. He looks fifteen."

"Ted told David where to go to get a fake ID."

"Tell them to be careful."

"Miriam, take a selfie with your iPad. Something to remember you by."

She leaned back, snapped the picture and texted it to him.

"Come on, I miss you. Show a bit more. Take off the tee shirt."

She hesitated momentarily, but then thought, *what is the big deal. He has seen me in my underwear.* She took off the tee shirt and sat on the bed in only her panties and a bra. In an instant he had a picture of her.

"You look beautiful. But how about a bit more. Take off the underwear. Let me see you the way God made you."

"No way."

Kevin could be charming, and persuasive. She had been attracted to him since they met at a youth group dance two years ago. He was two years older and seemed vastly more mature to her. Now he spoke gently. "Miriam, eventually you will get naked in front of me. I miss you. I don't want to look at all these other girls, as beautiful as they are. It is between us. No one will know."

Miriam hesitated another second. She loved Kevin but was constantly saying *no* to him. She was sure that those college girls were not shy about getting naked in front of him. This seemed like a little thing. She removed her underwear, held the iPad up away from her, and snapped the selfie. In a moment, Miriam Pollack, the daughter of the synagogue president, the shy girl who had to be drawn out of her shell for her bat mitzvah, had sent a nude picture of herself onto the internet. Sure, it was for Kevin's eyes only. The minute she sent it, she regretted it. But it was too late. "Got to go," she said nervously. "See you next week."

The Eastman Jewish Academy High School had an assembly about once a month, immediately after homeroom. More than 100 ninth to twelfth graders took seats in the auditorium. Dr. Judith Baker led the pledge of allegiance, and the students sang the Star-Spangled Banner and Hatikvah, Israel's national anthem. Then Dr. Baker called up Rabbi Lebovic to give a *d'var Torah*, a word of Torah. This was the norm at every assembly. The rabbi spoke about how, in the Garden of Eden, Adam and Eve were vegetarians. "Good for them," shouted David Eisenberg, but Dr. Baker hushed him. The rabbi continued with the divine permission to eat meat, given only after Noah and the flood. David turned to Joshua sitting next to him, "First Noah saves the animals, then he kills them." Joshua drove his elbow into David's side.

Next was an award ceremony for the girls' volleyball team:. first place in the private school division. Joshua's younger sister Shira was on the team, although she was only a freshman. He was proud of his sister as she went up to get her medal. Shira had all the athletic ability in the family; Joshua could barely throw a baseball. As a young girl she had been a gymnast, but she could not compete because most of the competitions were on Saturday. Rabbi Williams would not allow his kids to compete on the Jewish Sabbath. But now in high school she played volleyball and soccer, and in the spring hoped to join the girls' track team. The auditorium applauded the winning volleyball team.

Finally, Dr. Baker returned to the podium with some exciting news. "Many of you have heard about the academic fair competition. Groups of students submit projects in any academic field – science, social science, humanities. We had our own mini-fair here on campus. The faculty submitted one entry to the state competition in the state capitol. Our school was invited to compete in the statewide academic fair. Let me invite up to speak about their project – Joshua Williams, Heather Hall, and Lewis Reynolds. Their project – *Memes and Natural Selection.*"

Joshua was truly surprised. He did not think the project was that good. He had been assigned to work with Heather and Lewis, neither of whom he was particularly close to. Fortunately, Lewis had the reputation of being the most intelligent student in the senior class. He also came from the most religious home. An African American, Lewis along with his family had converted to Judaism when he was five. They had been Evangelical Christians but wanted to learn more about the religion of Jesus. At first they moved to a Messianic congregation, but that was more Christianity than Judaism. They then moved to the local Chabad, where Lewis's parents studied for two years. The Chabad rabbi would not convert them, so they turned to Joshua's father. Rabbi Williams converted the entire family, and they became some of his most active members of his synagogue, attending every Friday night and every Saturday morning. Lewis bragged about how he went through a full circumcision when he was five years old.

Lewis took the microphone, much to Joshua's relief. Joshua

knew that he was not a public speaker, unlike his dad who could give a sermon to a full congregation on Yom Kippur. In fact, Joshua had trouble finding anything he was good at. He was an average student with average looks and no particular talents he could speak of, unless one counted being good at video games. Lewis, far too articulate for a high school senior, described their project.

"We all learned in biology about evolution through natural selection. Certain biological traits are passed down through generations and survive, while other biological traits disappear. The ones that survive are the ones that give a benefit to the organism. The basic unit of biological survival is the gene. Genes are passed down from generation to generation. It is a fact of biology." So far Lewis sounded impressive.

"Animals live in a world of biology, in nature. Humans on the other hand, live in a world of culture. Culture is passed down from generation to generation. Culture – from religion to laws to government to art and music – differentiates humans from animals. How do we pass on culture from generation to generation? Dr. Richard Dawkins invented a term called a *meme*. A meme is a bit of cultural information, parallel to a gene. What a gene is to biology, a meme is to culture."

Shmuel Stern, newly Orthodox, shouted out. "Why are you talking about Dawkins? I thought he hates religion. He does not belong in a Jewish Day School."

Lewis looked at him. "Yes, he hates religion. But we can still learn from him. And his idea of the meme has passed into our general culture. The question we studied is, are memes subject to natural selection within a culture, like genes? Do memes either survive or disappear over the course of generations? Let me let one of my colleagues talk. Heather?"

Heather nervously took the microphone and Joshua felt relief. "Fortunately, with the help of the internet, we studied various memes over various years, to see if they were growing or shrinking. We looked at the number of times a meme is mentioned on Google, and the years it is mentioned. For example, to look at a meme that has survived for hundreds of years, we looked Shakespeare's words from Hamlet, *To be or not to be, that is the question.* Millions and millions of hits, continuing to grow from year to year. Then we looked at a meme from World War II I learned from my grandmother. *Loose lips sink ships.* It seemed to be shrinking and disappearing. Hardly anybody has quoted it in the last few years. Finally, we looked at a relatively new meme from the television show *Game of Thrones*: *You Win or You Die.* It is growing every year, moving beyond the television show into the general culture. In the same way, we studied several dozen cultural memes."

Lewis took over again. "Our conclusion. Human culture is subject to the same type of natural selection as nature. Genes flourish or disappear in nature, and memes flourish or disappear in a culture."

The students applauded.

Joshua went back to sit down, relieved that he did not have to speak. Dr. Baker spoke again. "Our three students will go to the state capital to present their findings at the academic fair competition. The top three in each state will go on to the national competition in Washington D.C. Next Monday and Tuesday I hope you will cheer on our three students as they participate in this competition."

This is the first time Joshua heard that he would be going out of town. Dr. Baker would be joining them. He imagined that he and Lewis would share a hotel room, Heather would have her own room as would Dr. Baker. It dawned on him that next Monday he would miss his father's sex class. He was a bit disappointed.

6. THIRD CLASS
COVERING NAKEDNESS

I only had sixteen students in my third class. Three students including my son had gone to the state capital for the academic fair and one student was sick. This class covered some particularly important material. I was hoping that the school would allow a make-up session with these four students.

Before I even began, Gary Brown spoke out, "You promised to tell us why humans are different from animals. According to everything we learned in biology, there is no essential difference. We share common ancestors and a common genetic code. We are simply fancy animals with more complex brains. If science is true, how can you say that we are different?"

I knew that the question whether science is true would take me far afield from the topic of the day. "Science can give us the best explanation for natural phenomenon. Science explains the things of nature. But religion speaks about issues that go beyond nature: spiritual matters. Science does not deal with these."

Gary replied, "So, religion is only about the supernatural? No wonder it is nonsense." Several students seemed impatient with Gary's arguments, but I needed to reply.

"Who says it is nonsense? Science can tell you how life evolved, but it cannot tell you why life evolved. Science can tell you how life works but it cannot tell you why life is important. For some questions, you need religion. Or else all of nature is *filled with sound and fury signifying nothing.*" It felt good to quote Shakespeare's *Macbeth*. My son had done his academic project on memes, and this was one of my favorite memes. It let the class know that my knowledge is not limited to religion. "So what is the difference between humans and animals? I want to quote the second creation story in the Torah."

Katy immediately asked, "There are two creation stories?"

"Yes, there is the first chapter of Genesis which speaks of six days of creation. And there is the second and third chapters of Genesis which speak of Adam and Eve and the Tree of Knowledge of Good and Evil. They are two very different stories."

Again, Gary interrupted me. "You don't believe that story is true, do you?" I think Gary was trying to annoy me, but I love being challenged on issues of religion and science. It is one of my favorite topics.

"Gary, there is literal truth, scientific truth. Then there is mythical truth. It is a myth that teaches us truths about the universe. What is the truth that the story of Adam and Eve teaches?"

Katy answered, "It teaches about the fall of man. I know

what they say, *By Adam's fall, sinners all.*" Memes seem important to this class.

"That is exactly what Christians would say. It is about the fall of man, about original sin. Jews reject that idea. What if I tell you that it is not the story of the *fall* of man but of the *rise* of man?"

Now I had their attention.

I continued, "It says that when Adam and Eve were in the Garden of Eden, they were naked and not ashamed. Who runs around naked and not ashamed?"

I heard several answers all at once. "Young children." "People at a nudist colony." Finally, someone said "animals."

"Correct, it is the story of when we were animals. Animals are naked and not ashamed. Now imagine you put a dog biscuit in front of your dog and say, *don't eat it.* What would your dog do?"

"Eat it anyway."

"Of course. Animals follow their appetites. That is what we spoke about two weeks ago when we said animals have one *yetzer*. God put the Tree of Knowledge of Good and Evil in the Garden, expecting full well that Adam and Eve would eventually eat from it. And when Eve took the fruit – by the way, nowhere does it say that it was an apple – and then gave the fruit to Adam, what was the first thing they realized?"

Katy seemed to bounce in her seat, anxious to answer, "They were naked and embarrassed."

"Correct, they were naked. They had to cover themselves up with fig leaves. Later God made animals skins to cover them up.

They were no longer animals; they could use the skins of animals because they were no longer their cousins. Their status changed. It is a story of evolution. It is the evolution of humans from being animals to being something more. And when they became something more, they started covering themselves up. This is part of how humans differentiate themselves from the animal kingdom. But why the cover up?"

I could hear noises up the hall, so I paused for a moment. I then asked a question that would introduce my main theme. "Tell me, suppose you were to walk into synagogue and nobody else was around. Suppose the Torah scroll was lying there open. What would you do?"

Almost all the students answered at once. They were familiar with the realities of the synagogue practices. "We would cover it up."

"Correct. You all know that the Torah needs to be covered up. It is only uncovered when we read it, then it is covered once again. Why?"

I waited but there was no answer. Finally, I motioned as if I was covering the Torah, "We cover up the Torah because it is a holy object. Part of how we show that something is holy is by covering it up. Back in the ancient Tabernacle, the holiest place was covered by a permanent curtain. Even today we hang a curtain in front of the ark where we keep the Torah scrolls. Covering up is our way of showing that something is holy.

"So it is with human beings. We are holy. And we show our

holiness by covering up. Does anyone know the phrase the Torah uses when it wants to talk about improper sexual relations?"

Shmuel eagerly answered, "Rabbi Lebovic uses the phrase *gilui arayot*."

I smiled, "Correct. *Gilui arayot* means uncover the nakedness. For example, we read on Yom Kippur, *The nakedness of your father and the nakedness of your mother you shall not uncover, she is your mother, do not uncover her nakedness.* Judaism is very concerned with covering up."

I continued, "Anybody know what *tzniyot* is?"

Shmuel continued, "Modesty, keeping yourself covered up. Rabbi Lebovic talks about it all the time. Only he uses the phrase *tzniyus*."

I explained, "Rabbi Lebovic uses the old Ashkenazic pronunciation. I use the modern Israeli pronunciation. But it is the same word. *Tzniyot* means modesty or covering up."

Miriam Pollack spoke. "Does this mean we have to cover up with long sleeves and long dresses like Rabbi Lebovic's daughters? Does it mean that the boys have to wear those long black coats like Rabbi Lebovic?"

"No," I answered, "Different cultures have different definitions of what it means to cover up. I have no problem with women wearing pants, wearing short sleeves, men wearing shorts. But there are still parts of the body that ought to be covered when in public."

Now it was time for the key question. "When is it okay to uncover yourself to someone else? Do you wait until you are married? Do you wait until you are engaged? Do you wait until you are in love? Do you wait until college, or do you uncover yourself for someone in high school? Do you uncover on the first date? Do you uncover yourself to someone you picked up at a party? When is it okay to uncover yourself for someone?"

Katy spoke with sadness in her voice. "I think my parents should have uncovered themselves sooner. My dad lived out of town and my mom came from a very old-fashioned home. My dad visited and romanced my mom. But they never lived together. I do not even know if they had sex until they married. By the time they did marry, the relationship went downhill quickly. Maybe they should have spent more time together, seeing each others' nakedness, before they married. Probably they would not have married. But then of course, I would not have been born."

Several students nodded their heads sympathetically. Katy seemed to be unburdening herself with her words. These students had known her since she was young and were aware of her parents' difficult marriage and divorce.

Miriam then asked me, "Do you think couples should live together before they are married?"

"Let me save that question to a later class. For now, let me say that our job is to be different from the animals. Animals are naked and not ashamed. Humans cover up, until they choose to uncover for someone." I closed my notes and stood up. "The question to think about is, when do you think it is okay to uncover for someone else? The secondary question is, are high school students ready to

72

uncover themselves for someone else? Think about it for next week."

This time they seemed to leave the room more slowly.

7. THE HOTEL ROOM

"I can't believe I told the entire class that my parents should not have gotten married. What made me share that? I even told the rabbi. It is as if the words poured out of me before I could stop myself." Nicolas and Katy were sitting in Starbucks at the mall, their regular meeting place. Luckily no one but Nicolas saw the tears in Katy's eyes.

Nicolas took Katy's hand in his own. "You did nothing wrong. I know you are upset, not only by your parents' divorce, but the way they treat each other. Sometimes you have to talk about it."

Katy continued, "I actually said that my parents should have lived together before they got married. Maybe they would have gotten to know each other better. Maybe they would have realized that it was not a good marriage. Do you think couples should live together before they get married?"

"I don't know," said Nicolas. "My parents would never approve. They are old-fashioned Catholics who believe that sex belongs only in marriage. They also believe that sex should only be to have babies. If I lived with a girlfriend, or even a fiancée before

I married, they would not approve. They may not cut me off, but they would not approve."

Katy looked him in the eye, "When I get married, I plan to live with my fiancée. I would want to know if we were compatible. I don't ever want to go through what my parents went through." Then she changed the subject, "Nicolas, did you study the story of Adam and Eve in your school?"

"When I was much younger. The nuns taught that this is the story of original sin. It is how sin came into the world. When Adam ate from the apple ..."

Katy interrupted him, "It never says that it was an apple."

He continued, "The nuns said it was an apple. When Adam ate from the apple, humanity fell from God's grace. We all became sinners. We talked a lot about original sin. We are now all sinners. It took the death of Jesus to bring us out of our state of sin, to bring us back into God's good graces. Of course, we still have to go to mass and attend confessionals. But the nuns talk a lot about original sin because it is one of the most important Catholic ideas."

"Jews don't believe in original sin."

"Really. How do you explain the story of Adam and Eve?"

"Rabbi Williams actually taught that eating from the fruit was a good thing. He called it the rise of man, not the fall of man. He says that it is a mythical story of how we rose above the animals. It was almost as if Darwin wrote the story. Evolution of humanity was that moment when we realized that we were no longer animals, we were naked and ashamed. As Rabbi Williams explained it, God wanted us to eat from the fruit. He planted the tree with the realization that we were animals, and animals cannot resist temptation. We ate and became human."

Nicolas stared at her for the moment. "That sounds crazy. I never heard such an interpretation. Do all Jews believe that?"

"I remember Rabbi Lebovic saying that Adam sinned and deserved to be punished. But he is an Orthodox rabbi and Rabbi Williams is a more liberal rabbi. I think only a liberal rabbi can say that eating the forbidden fruit was a good thing."

"If it is a good thing, why were Adam and Eve punished? If I remember, Eve would have pain in childbirth. And Adam was taught that by the sweat of his brow he would eat bread. Why punish a good thing?"

Katy thought for a second. "Maybe it was less a punishment than a description of the difference between animals and humans. Animals have an easier time giving birth than humans, because we humans have such big heads. It is very hard to fit a human head through the birth canal. That is why so many women used to die in childbirth."

"They still do."

"Not like in the past. The big brains which give us such big heads are exactly what makes childbirth so dangerous. And animals seem to provide for themselves by instinct. The food they need is out there. Humans must work for bread. In fact, bread doesn't grow on trees. We have to harvest wheat and separate it and grind it into flour and knead it, and only then bake it. My mother and I sometimes bake bread together. No animal has to do all that."

Nicolas looked her in the eye. "You know, you would probably make a pretty good rabbi yourself." For the first time that day, Katy smiled. Again, Nicolas leaned over and kissed her. Both of them knew that, although he was only allowed to date Catholics and she was only allowed to date Jews, this was getting serious. They really liked each other. Neither dared admit to their parents that they were seeing one another. They would text and chat, but only meet face-to-face at the mall.

Monday afternoon Joshua, Lewis, and Heather, together with Dr. Baker, returned to the hotel. It was a successful if long day. They had presented their project to two sets of judges and listened to multiple other presentations of students from throughout the state. Tomorrow, the judges would pick ten projects to make one more presentation, before choosing first, second, and third place awards. Those would go on to Washington D.C. Joshua was not sure he even wanted to win. He felt relief that he did not have to do much talking. Lewis led much of the presentation with Heather adding her thoughts now and again. Joshua only spoke during the initial introduction.

Dr. Baker ordered a pizza which they ate in the hotel lobby. Then she returned to her room and asked them not to disturb her. She was exhausted. Heather returned to her room and Lewis and Joshua sat in the lobby playing a game of chess. Then they went up the elevator to their room and turned on the television. Dr. Baker wanted them to meet downstairs at 8 am for the second day of the contest.

An hour later the phone rang in their hotel room. Joshua picked up to hear Heather's voice. "Can you come over for a moment? Be quiet, I don't want Dr. Baker to know that you are in my room."

"I will be right there." He quietly passed by Dr. Baker's room and knocked on Heather's door. She quickly let him in. She had changed out of the conservative dress from the conference to a pair of cut-off shorts and a tee shirt. "Joshua, have a seat on the bed."

He sat a bit confused. What did she want? Heather sat next to him and took his hand. "You are so quiet. You let me and Lewis do all the talking. I have always liked guys who are quiet and reserved. Maybe because I am so talkative. We have been together in that school for years, but I have never gotten to know you. I know you are the rabbi's son. But who are you?"

Joshua's mouth was dry, his tongue felt stiff, and he could not breathe. Heather moved a bit closer and touched his leg. "If you are not going to talk, then I will tell you something about me. You know that I have an older brother named Marc. He is a junior in college. I remember something my mom said to him before he went off to college. My mom told Marc that a boy ought to be experienced. He should try to sow his oats when he could. My mom actually said that to him. But she continued, *then when you are ready to get married, marry a girl without sexual experience.* You want to teach her. If you do that, you will have a better marriage."

Joshua asked, "She didn't really say that?"

Heather moved her hand up his leg. "She did. I was still young. but challenged my mom. She did not know I was listening. Why should girls be different than boys? Why should boys sow their oats while girls wait passively? I made a decision that day. *What is good for the goose is good for the gander.* If boys can be sexually experienced, so can girls. A few months later, I went on the pill."

Joshua tensed up. "Why are you telling me this?"

Heather continued, "I have always liked you. But I always thought you were unavailable, being the rabbi's son and all. But now I know you are like every other boy in our school. You want it, but maybe you are a bit scared. We are out of town. Your daddy is not around."

Heather took off her top. She was not wearing a bra and Joshua noticed the perfect shape of her breasts. "Lie back," she ordered. He could only obey. What happened next was quick, almost too quick to be enjoyable. It took perhaps five minutes for Joshua to lose his virginity. He lay back, feeling a mix of feelings, a tiredness tied to an exhilaration. He had thought about how to lose his virginity, but he never thought it would be to Heather. If Miriam was the prettiest girl in the senior class, Heather was the sexiest. Often when the boys were alone they spoke about the way she dressed, her outgoing personality, and her strident feminism. Many boys said they would like to have sex with her.

"Lewis is going to wonder what happened to me." Joshua went to the bathroom to clean himself and put his clothes on. Heather lay on the bed naked. "Did you know that you are number five?"

"Number five?"

"Yes. It is my personal project. I want to help the boys at the Eastman Jewish Academy become men. You are the fifth boy who lost his virginity to me. I believe that I am doing a great mitzvah, helping boys be ready for college. Joshua, I like you but don't misinterpret this. I am not looking for a relationship. I don't think I am capable of an ongoing relationship. But I do really like you."

Joshua gave her a quick kiss and returned to his room. Lewis was still watching television. "What did she want?"

"Some question about homework." Joshua wondered whether Lewis was one of the boys that Heather had helped become a man. He doubted it. Lewis's parents were deeply religious, and sex outside of marriage was utterly forbidden. But perhaps more notably – Joshua couldn't believe he was even thinking this way, but Lewis was black. He had never thought of Lewis ethinically first. But now that he had lost his virginity, maybe it was the call of his DNA that was surfacing, and he couldn't help but wonder: would Heather have sex with a black man? Joshua climbed into bed but could not fall asleep for a long time.

Several days later, Isar and Joshua sat in Isar's bedroom playing video games. They did this several days a week. Isar's parents were rarely home, working long hours at the flea market, and Isar was an only child. There was nobody around to bother them. Joshua had a strange smirk on his face. Isar finally asked him, "Why are you smiling like that?'

He replied, "Isar, you are looking at someone new. I am no longer a boy anymore. I am now a man."

"I thought you became a man at your bar mitzvah."

"Seriously, I am now a man. I lost my virginity this week."

"How? With whom? You don't even have a girlfriend."

"Isar, you do not need a girlfriend to lose your virginity. In fact, it is probably easier if you don't have a girlfriend. Too many complications."

Isar looked at him strangely. "Let me guess. You hired a prostitute. Like that one in that story your dad told in class. Six mattresses of silver and one of gold."

"It was no prostitute. In fact, it was a girl from this school."

"No way. You lost your virginity to a nice Jewish girl who goes to a private Jewish school? No way. Who?"

Joshua smiled, "Who do you think? Who is the sexiest girl in the school?"

"Heather Hall! Can't be. The one who is always spouting off about feminism. I thought she was a lesbian the way she talks."

"She is as straight as they come."

Isar started to question him. "This must have happened when you were at the state capital. You two shared a hotel room?"

"No, Lewis and I shared a hotel room. She invited me to her room when Dr. Baker was asleep. It happened so quickly. She was talking to me and before I knew it, my pants were down she was on top of me. You know what she told me? Her mom told her older brother to sow his wild oats. But as a girl, she should remain a virgin until she gets married. Heather's too strong a feminist to ever agree to that. She immediately went on birth control."

Joshua continued, "She told me that she had a project in mind. Her goal was to help all the senior boys at our school lose their virginity before they go to college. She told me I was the fifth boy from our class. The only problem is that within a minute, it was over."

Isar was incredulous. "No way. How do I set up an appointment with her?"

"From what I can see, you wait till she finds you."

Isar raised his hand. "Fist bump. This is a cause for celebration. Joshua, the overprotected rabbi's son, is no longer a virgin. This calls for a drink. Come on, I know where my dad hides the scotch."

By the time Isar's parents got home, the two boys had gone through half a bottle of Scotch. Fortunately, the parents were too tired to notice.

8. FOURTH CLASS
PRIVACY

The next Monday I had perfect attendance. My son seemed in a good mood, laughing and joking with his friend Isar as they entered the class. I looked at the other students. All seemed happy. Joshua's team did not win the academic fair but they placed in the top ten. They would not be going to Washington D.C. for the national fair. Not surprisedly, when my son heard, he seemed relieved.

Most the students were talking and joking. The only one who seemed serious if not outright glum was Barry Pollack's daughter Miriam. In fact, she seemed sad, on the verge of tears. Her friend Katy was trying to cheer her up without success. I had known these two girls since they were young children and I wondered if I could somehow help them. But I had to respect their privacy. I wondered if Miriam was still seeing the college kid – what was his name – Kevin. It was time to start the class.

"Anyone know the verse from the Torah that we say we enter a synagogue? "

There was a moment of silence until Shlomo spoke out,

״מַה־טֹּבוּ אֹהָלֶיךָ יַעֲקֹב מִשְׁכְּנֹתֶיךָ יִשְׂרָאֵל:

Mah Tovu.

How goodly are your tents O Jacob, your dwelling places O Israel (Numbers 24:5)."

"Good, and who said those words originally?"

Shlomo responded, "Balaam."

Good, I thought, after twelve years of religious school, someone knows the answer to a basic question from the Torah.

I smiled, "Correct. The words were spoken by a non-Jew, Balaam. You know him, the one whose donkey talked back to him. He was hired by Balak the King of Moab to curse the Jews. But God changed the curses into blessings. This blessing was so important that the rabbis chose it to be said when walking into a synagogue."

I continued. "You may wonder what this has to do with sexual ethics. Let me share what the Midrash says about this verse. Why were the households of Israel so beautiful, considering they were temporary tents the Israelites erected in the desert? The Rabbis said that there were 600,000 tents in the desert, and they were set up in a way that no door faced any other door, no window faced any other window. Why was that important?"

Again Shlomo spoke up. "There was absolute privacy."

"Good. The rabbis were concerned about the value of privacy.

Remember the quote invented by some ad agency, *What happens in Vegas stays in Vegas.* It has become a popular meme. Generations before that saying, the Rabbis taught, what happens in one's home stays in one's home. Even more importantly, what happens in the bedroom stays in the bedroom. Too often today we lose sight of the difference between the private and the public. We discuss things with friends that should be private. We put things on social media that should be private. All this is related to what we spoke about last week, holiness begins with keeping things covered."

I continued. "Suppose a boy in this school decides to have sex with a girl in this school. Do you think they will keep it private?"

Heather suddenly burst out laughing; I wondered what was going through her mind.

"Heather, do you think they will keep it private?"

Heather responded, "Boys like to brag. I imagine that a boy would tell all his friends."

"And what about girls?"

"Girls can be more catty. The girl may try to keep it a secret. But her girlfriends will find out." Again she started laughing.

"Heather, is there something you want to share with the class?"

"O no rabbi, I believe in keeping things private." Now the class started laughing - everyone but Miriam.

I rolled my eyes but enjoyed Heather's wit. "Judaism has other laws about privacy. Tell me, at a Jewish wedding, immediately after the ceremony, what do the bride and groom do?"

This time David spoke up, "They form a receiving line."

"Not at a Jewish wedding. They go into a secluded room together. It is called *yichud*. In the Orthodox world they put two witnesses outside the door to make sure no one bothers them. There was a time when they literally consummated the marriage." Again laughter filled the room. "Today it is more symbolic. But by Jewish tradition, an unmarried man and woman were not allowed to be alone in a room together. Most of us outside the Orthodox world no longer observe that strictly. But there is something powerful in the symbolism of being alone together for the first time."

Lewis raised his hand. "Do you observe that tradition?"

"I will tell you what I do. I make a point of never being alone with a woman in my office or anywhere else with the door closed. I know too many rabbis who have gotten in trouble. There should never be the suspicion of anything unseemly."

Miriam spoke out. "What if you are counseling a woman about something really private? Do you still keep the door open?"

"I do. People cannot hear what we say. But with the door open there is not even the appearance of improper behavior." I wondered if there was something Miriam wanted to discuss with me. It was time to mention something I wanted to say at the beginning. "We are discussing a lot of personal matters in this class: homosexuality, abortion, masturbation, and of course, teen age sex. If anyone ever has something they want to discuss with me, I will listen to you. All discussions with a rabbi are confidential. There is one exception. If I believe you are a threat to yourself or someone else, for example, if you tell me that you are considering suicide, I cannot keep that private. But anything else is confidential."

Katy said, "You won't tell our parents?"

"I won't even tell your parents. Whatever people share with me is private."

Katy spoke up again. "Rabbi, when someone tells something to a Catholic priest at confession, don't they have to keep it secret? Even if they are threatening suicide."

"In the Catholic Church, the confession is a holy sacrament, one of seven holy sacraments. The priest is bound by certain vows to uphold the privacy of that sacrament. Rabbis are not priests and we take no such vows. But we do have certain professional ethics we must uphold. One is the privacy and confidentiality of all communication. Again, that is only if no one is being threatened by harm." I paused, looking around the class, wondering what kind of issues these students might be willing to share with me.

"Let us return to our topic – the Jewish value of privacy. What is the biggest threat to privacy today?"

I watched the class ponder the question. Then David called out, "Social media."

I nodded. "Good. The biggest threat to privacy is the internet, social media, Facebook, Twitter, Instagram, Snapchat, Ticktock, others that you know about that I am sure I never heard of. People post things on the Internet that ought to be in the realm of privacy. There are no secrets and no realm of privacy in the world of social media. Let me share a warning with you. When you apply for a job, your potential employer will look you up on social media.

If there are videos of you on Facebook acting drunk or posing in a sexually explicit way, it could threaten your job. You need to have a realm of privacy.

"Let me give you an assignment. When you get home I want you to go on social media and ask the question, is this something I want my employer to see? Is this something I want my college recruiter to see? Is this something I want my future wife or husband to see? If you can, take it off. Or better, do not put it up in the first place. Social media submissions are often impossible to remove. The tents of ancient Israel were holy because they respected each other's privacy." I finally ended. I felt a little bad, it was more of a sermon than a class. But these high school seniors needed to hear it. "Class dismissed."

When class was over, Miriam came up to me. "Rabbi, can I talk to you privately?"

"Of course."

"Do we need to keep the classroom door open?"

"Yes, but no one can hear us."

"And you will keep this confidential. I know my dad is president of the synagogue. Will you tell him?"

"I will not tell anyone – unless you are thinking of harming yourself or someone else." I had to include that caveat. "Miriam, you look very sad."

"Rabbi, I did what you warned us not to do. I know you heard that I am dating a college boy named Kevin. We met several years ago at a youth group dance. Don't worry rabbi, he is Jewish. In fact, he grew up in our synagogue. I am embarrassed to say this. I snapped a picture of myself in the nude and sent it to him. I don't know why. I was lonely and he pushed me. The minute I did it I wanted to take it back."

"Has he shown the picture to others?"

"He said he loves me. He would not do that."

"Miriam, if he loves you, truly loves you as you say, why would he push you to do something that you are not comfortable with? Why would he push you to do something that goes against your values?"

"I thought all boys do that. They push their girlfriends."

"Miriam, a boy who truly loves a girl will think about her needs, her comfort. He will not put pressure on you to do what you do not want to do. Hopefully the picture is still private, not out on social media. You can ask him to erase the picture. Maybe, if he really respects you, he will. In the future, I want you to think about what we taught about a realm of privacy and staying covered up."

"Thank you, rabbi. You won't tell my parents."

"Your secret is safe with me." She smiled as she left. But I had a bad feeling. Knowing college boys the way I do, I sensed her secret would not stay secret for long.

9. THE GAY BAR

On Saturday evening Katy and Nicolas sat on the bed in Katy's bedroom. Her mom was out on a date, which made Katy happy. Her mom was often depressed, having never fully recovered from the divorce from Katy's father. But she had met a man at work who asked her out to dinner. She needed someone new in her life. Katy knew her mom would be gone for several hours and felt safe inviting Nicolas to her home. She was still not allowed to date non-Jews, but this was not a date, just a chance to talk. Nicolas was the first religious Catholic Katy had ever met, and she enjoyed talking with him.

Katy said to him, "The issue of Catholic confession came up in my school on Monday. I am not sure the rabbi knows what he is talking about. What happens at a confession?"

"I go every month. You are in a kind of booth and the priest is behind a screen. You talk about your sins and the priest tells you what you need to do to find atonement. It used to be a lot of ritual. You know, do the Rosary or say *Out Father*. But I like it when the young priest is there. He acts more as a therapist than a clergy. You can talk to someone about your problems without paying $100 an hour."

"Have you mentioned me to him?"

"I mention everything to him. He has a great deal of respect for the Jewish people. He says Jesus was a Jew. He thinks it is wonderful that I am learning about Judaism from you."

"Would he ever mention me to your parents?"

Nicolas was astonished by the question. "It would be forbidden to talk to anyone about what happens in the confessional, even another priest. It is part of the sacrament. There must be absolute confidentiality. The priest took a sacred vow."

Katy continued. "Tell me, what if someone confessed to the priest that he was going to do something dangerous? What if someone confessed that they were going to commit suicide?"

"I am sure the priest would try to convince the person to seek help, to talk to a counselor or call a hotline. But it would be forbidden to reveal anything said at the confessional."

"What is someone confessed that they were going to commit a crime? What if they planned to murder someone?"

Nicolas smiled, "Katy, are you planning a murder?"

"Of course not. Our rabbi said that when people come to him for counseling, he must keep it confidential. He cannot tell anyone; if it is a teenager, he cannot even tell the parents. But he said the only exception is if they plan to harm themselves or others. If they are planning to kill themselves or someone else, he must tell."

"I am sure for the rabbi that he is following the ethical standards of his profession. But for the priest it is different. He has taken a vow, and the confession is a religious sacrament. It is one of seven sacred sacraments."

Katy responded, "What are the sacraments?"

Nicolas sat back. "Let's see, first there is baptism, which we Catholics perform on infants. Then there is communion, taking the Eucharist. I had my first communion when I was seven. There is confirmation for teenagers. I had that four years ago. There is confession. There is marriage. It used to be that the church would only recognize a marriage between two Catholics. Today I believe that the rules have been loosened. I can marry you one day in a church."

Katy started to giggle. "I don't think my parents would like it if a priest married me."

"He can co-officiate with your rabbi, Rabbi Williams."

"I don't think Rabbi Williams is allowed to do weddings with a priest. But aren't we rushing things a little?"

"Fair enough," said Nicolas. "Let's see, I mentioned baptism, communion, confirmation, confession, marriage. There are two more. One is holy order, when a priest takes his vows. And the other comes at the end of life, last rites, what they used to call extreme unction. Do Jews have anything similar at the end of life?"

"I know that Rabbi Williams goes to see people at the end of life. He says some kind of special prayer; he said it is called a *vidui*. Funny, that word means *confession*. I remember the rabbi talking about it once during a Yom Kippur sermon. He was talking about confessions in Judaism. He said that Catholics do confessions privately with a priest. Jews do confessions publicly on Yom Kippur. Ours are in the plural - *for the sins we committed.* For each sin we beat our chest."

"I am trying to imagine a thousand Jews beating their chests in unison."

"You should come on Yom Kippur. Anyway, the rabbi went on to say that there was a private *vidui* or confession right before death. If the person were conscious he or she would say it. But usually the dying person is not conscious, so the rabbi had to say it for them. I remember at the time thinking it was strange. It says - *may my death be an atonement for all my sins.*"

"I guess we need to face our Maker free of sins."

"Nicolas, do you believe we go to heaven when we die?"

"I do, assuming we are free of sins. Unfortunately, we live in a world filled with opportunities to sin." As if to prove his point, Nicolas leaned over and kissed her.

After a deep kiss, Katy sat back and said, "Would your priest approve?"

"He is not here. I will confess it next week. Your mom is not here either." Nicolas began to unbutton her blouse, and then fumbled trying to unhook her bra. She really liked Nicolas and decided to help him along. He and she were both inexperienced, but one thing quickly led to another. Soon they were embracing each other, naked in her bed. And then he was inside her, where he came quicker than she expected. It hurt a little, but she heard that it always hurt the first time. And so Katy, who had never even had a boyfriend, lost her virginity to a boy she was not even allowed to date.

After lying back for a few moments, Nicolas turned to her. "I am sorry, Katy. I did not mean for that to happen. But I really love you."

"I did not expect that to happen either. But I am glad it did. Have you ever gone all the way with a girl before?"

"Making out. But not all the way. I am glad I did it for the first time with you."

"I have never even made out with a boy. In fact, I have never had a boy who liked me. But I am glad we did it. There is one thing that is a relief. I heard from my girlfriend that when you do it for the first time, you can't get pregnant."

The same Saturday evening that Katy lost her virginity, Miriam decided to protect hers. After her conversation with Rabbi Williams, she decided that she was not ready to go all the way with Kevin. It was a decision that would come to haunt her.

Kevin and Miriam went to the movies. Then they went over to Kevin's home. His parents were out for the evening, and his roommate Ted who was staying with him had gone with David to some gay bar that had opened downtown. Again, Miriam lied to her parents, saying she was with Katy. In truth, Miriam and Katy hardly saw each other outside of school. She was spending all her time with Nicolas, the boy she had met at the party. That saddened Miriam. She could use Katy's friendship right now. She was no longer comfortable being alone in the house with Kevin.

The moment they arrived home Kevin grabbed her to kiss her. She pulled back. "Kevin, stop." He continued to pull her towards him. "Kevin, please stop!" she said more emphatically. He pulled her towards him even harder. "Kevin, I said stop!" When he would not let go, she slapped him.

He looked shocked. "Miriam, what are you doing?"

"I am not in the mood right now. Sorry, Kevin."

"What's going on, Miriam? A few weeks ago you send me a picture of you totally nude. Now you won't let me kiss you. I don't understand."

"It is the picture. I believe it was a mistake. I should not have sent it."

"Miriam, that picture allows me to tolerate being separated from you when I am away at school. I look at it, think of you, and I am no longer lonely."

"I want you to destroy that picture."

"Miriam, I am not going to destroy that picture. I need that picture. What is the big deal? You are beautiful. I have seen you in a swimsuit. I have seen you in your underwear. Now I have seen you *au natural,* the way God made you. Tonight I planned to see you in person that way. Look what I brought." Kevin took out a box of condoms. "Tonight will be special. I planned for us to finally go all the way. I love you, and I know that you love me. It is time to celebrate this love."

Miriam looked shocked. "You did not ask me what I planned. What if I do not want to go all the way? What if I want to wait?"

"Wait for what Miriam? Wait till we're old and gray. Wait till we're married. How long am I supposed to wait? All the guys in my college are sexually active. All but me. I figured that if you are willing to strip down for me for a photograph, you would do it in person. If you love me, you would not make me wait."

"Kevin, you know that I am in Rabbi William's sex class. The rabbi says that animals go about naked. Humans keep themselves covered, until they are absolutely sure for whom they want to uncover themselves. I am not ready to uncover myself, with you or with anyone."

"You are going to let a rabbi keep us apart." He clenched his fists as he growled, "Why have you led me on all these months?"

Kevin tried to grab her and kiss her again. Again she slapped him, even harder this time. His face stung. He rubbed his cheek and shouted at her, calling her horrible names.

She had never seen him angry like this. She started to shake. "Kevin, take me home."

"Miriam, find your own way home."

Miriam walked out the door and Kevin slammed it behind her. She stood there several minutes with tears in her eyes – angry, frightened, not sure what to do. Then she did the one thing she dreaded. She called her dad and asked him to come pick her up.

She had lied to her parents. Now she would have to face her father's wrath.

When she arrived home she saw that Kevin had texted her. She ignored it. He kept texting her, at least 20 times. "Miriam, I am sorry. Miriam, let's talk. Miriam, if you want to wait, I will wait." "Miriam, I love you." She ignored the texts. Then he started calling; over and over the phone rang.

Finally she swiped up. "Kevin, stop it. I think we need to take some time apart for a while."

"Miriam, don't do this. Please." She thought of the terrible things he said to her. She thought of his refusal to drive her home. She thought of his buying condoms and just assuming she would go all the way. Was this the boy she wanted to uncover her nakedness to? But she had already uncovered her nakedness, at least in a photograph. She felt this deep sense of shame.

He called once more, and she answered him for the last time. "Kevin, please leave me alone. Do not call me. Do not text me. I need time apart." She hung up and blocked him, relieved that the phone was silent. Miriam tried to call her friend Katy but there was no answer. She lay in bed crying for a long time before she finally fell asleep.

The Bitter End, the name of the new gay nightclub, was lit up and the parking lot was full. The club was in the middle of the downtown entertainment district. Multiple bars and restaurants were crowded with young people out on a Saturday night. David Eisenberg had gone by Uber with Ted Armstrong, excited and nervous. When they approached the burly security guard at the entrance, he barely glanced at David's fake id. He was too busy looking at Ted. In fact, many eyes turned to look at Ted. He was tall with a muscular physique and handsome features. David felt absolutely inadequate next to Ted, scrawny with his horn-rimmed glasses and the Jewish star around his neck, a gift from his grandmother which he never took off. As they walked through the entrance, David vowed to start going to the gym and build up his body. Perhaps he would also scrap the glasses and get contacts.

They sat down at the bar and ordered beers. Nobody asked his age. Ted ordered some chicken wings, and David looked at the menu to see if there was anything vegetarian. To be a vegetarian in a gay bar seemed incongruous. David ordered some French fries, avoiding asking his question whether they were fried in pure vegetable oil. If the chicken wings were fried in the same oil, he would have to live with it.

The music was loud and the lights were low. Many people were dancing. It was mostly men, unusually good-looking men. There were some women, many of whom seemed butch to David. There were also a few heterosexual couples. David wondered what they were doing there. Ted ate a few chicken wings and went off to mingle. It was clear to David that Ted would probably meet someone that night. As for him, he felt young and inadequate. He preferred to stay at the bar, nurse his beer and eat his French fries, and watch: so many good-looking men in one place.

The hours went by. David drank too many beers. He was glad he had not driven; if his car were there he would have been forced to call his parents to pick him up. And if his parents knew where he was, they would kill him. So David continued to watch the action, ordering more French fries and slowly getting drunk. Eventually, Ted walked over to him, a handsome young man clinging to his arm. The man had long blond hair and looked like he had just walked off the beach in Southern California, surfboard in hand. Ted said, "Listen buddy, it looks like I have some plans for tonight. I hope you don't mind taking an Uber home alone. I will catch up with you tomorrow." Ted giggled, looking like he had also had too many drinks. He then kissed the blond man.

"No problem," replied David. He looked at his watch. It was only ten o'clock. The night life was just beginning downtown. But David decided that he was ready to go home. Enough adventure for one night. He walked out to the parking lot, now somewhat deserted, and took out his cell phone to order an Uber.

David did not see the two men until they called out to him. "Hey, faggot," one of them called, and walked over to David. "Hey faggot, girls aren't good enough for you." The man had a shaved head and tattoos covered his arm. The other had a full head of hair and a heavy beard. The one with the beard walked to David and looked at his Jewish star. "Hey, Dean, look at this. This one is Jewish too. A faggot kike."

"Leave me alone."

The one with the beard took a handful of coins and threw them in front of David. "Let see if you are a Jew. Pick up the coins."

The one named Dean now walked over. "You know that Hitler killed the Jews. But Hitler also killed the fags. Do you think he would have killed you twice?"

"Leave me alone," shouted David. He turned to run from the two men, but someone held him back.

"Don't run from us. We're not done talking to you."

Tears welled up in David's eyes. He should not have gone to this gay bar, and he should not have gone out alone. How could he escape from these two? Dean put his face close to David. "Hey Bill, look at this one. He is crying. Do you want your mommy?" David was frozen. Dean held on to him.

Finally David was able to say, "What do you guys want?"

Bill came over and put his face close to David's. "What do we want? We want them to close this faggot bar. We are a moral town. We don't want this kind of thing in our town. Let the faggots go to San Francisco, or New York. We don't want your type coming here."

Dean continued, "We don't want faggots. And we don't want Jews. This is a town for good Christians."

"So let me get out of here. Let go of me." For a second David thought the two men were going to let him go. He would run as fast as he could. Then they heard police sirens. Someone, probably the security guard, must have called the police.

Dean screamed at Bill, "The Jew faggot called the police on

us."

Dean grabbed David even harder, "Why'd you call the police?"

"You saw me. I didn't call anyone."

The last thing David remembered was a fist smashing into his face. His glasses broke as he slumped to the ground unconscious. When he awoke an hour later, he was in a hospital.

10. FIFTH CLASS
SEX THAT HURTS

The students entered my class quieter than usual. Their thoughts must have been on their classmate David, still in the hospital. I knew that I must begin with this issue, "I received a call in the middle of the night Saturday night. As many of you know, the Eisenbergs are long time members of my synagogue. I officiated at their son David's bar mitzvah. David's parents told me that David was in the hospital, having been beaten up in front of a gay bar in the entertainment district. I immediately ran down to the hospital.

"David's nose was broken, and he had come out of surgery. He was also pretty banged up, with black eyes and horrible bruises on his face. In addition, his glasses were broken. When he awoke, he actually joked with me. He said that he knew it was time to get contacts. Thank God the doctor said he would be ok; he would just need time to heal. Anyway, it seems that David used a fake ID to get into a gay nightclub in the entertainment district. When he walked out to call an Uber, he was confronted by two thugs. They started insulting him for being gay, and for being Jewish. The security guard saw the confrontation and called 911. When they heard the police coming, the two of them beat David up.

"After I arrived the police came to question David. It seems that these two men were waiting outside the bar for a victim. Their names were Dean and Bill. And no, they did not know David. But he was alone outside a gay bar at night, wearing a Jewish star, so he seemed the perfect victim."

My mind wandered for a moment. I thought about Saturday night. I arrived home from the hospital after 2 am, surprised to see Marcia waiting up for me. "How is David?" I told her the story and how bad I felt for him and his family. Then she said something that surprised me. "Do you think your class had anything to do with what happened?"

I dismissed her concerns. "David would have gone to that gay bar, whether I was teaching a class or not."

Enough reliving Saturday night in my head. It was time to focus on my class.

Katy raised her hand, "Did they catch the guys who did this to David?"

"Not yet. But they have good descriptions from both David and the security guard. They are also checking the video cameras in the parking lot. They should catch them."

She continued, "If they did not know David, why would they pick on him? Why pick on a total stranger?"

I responded, "That seems to be the way of the world, to hate strangers, to hate those who are different. That is why through our long history, people have hated Jews. They have also hated blacks, foreigners, gypsies, Moslems, and in our day and age, gays. These two hated both gays and Jews. It seems almost natural to hate the other. Unfortunately, none of us are immune. For example, how do you feel when you meet a Jew with a long black coat, a black hat, and *payos*, the long side curls."

Gary Brown immediately spoke out. "I feel embarrassed that these people are Jews. Why can't they dress like everyone else, enter the modern world? Why do they insist on speaking Yiddish, a dead language?"

I looked at Gary, "Yiddish is hardly a dead language. It is spoken by hundreds of thousands of Hasidic and other Orthodox Jews. But think about your words. Here you are judging someone you do not even know. That is exactly what these two young men did to David Eisenberg. They knew nothing about him. All they knew is that he was at a gay bar and he was wearing a Jewish star. That was enough to beat him up."

I continued, "Do you know why we were slaves in Egypt for so many years? We were strangers, and the Torah wants us to learn to love the stranger. The Torah says it explicitly,

וַאֲהַבְתֶּם אֶת־הַגֵּר כִּי־גֵרִים הֱיִיתֶם בְּאֶרֶץ מִצְרָיִם

`Love the stranger, for you were strangers in the land of Egypt' (Deuteronomy 10:19).

"It is one of the great lessons our tradition has given the world. But too often we do not listen. Tell me, how do you feel when someone tells you that they are a fundamentalist, born again Christian?"

Again, Gary answered, "Uncomfortable. I don't like Bible thumpers."

"We are quick to judge. Maybe this fundamentalist, born again can become your closest friend. We need to love the stranger. It is part of the idea that every human being, whatever their race or religion or sexual orientation, is created in the image of God. Everyone deserves dignity."

Gary challenged me, "What about those two young men, what did you say their names were, Dean and Bill? They beat up my friend. Do I have to love them?"

I answered slowly, "I do not know what kind of background they come from that caused them to learn such hatred. I would love to sit and talk to them. I want to know what caused them to beat up an innocent seventeen-year-old boy."

Katy was surprised. "You would really want to talk with them?"

"I would. Our tradition teaches that people can change. Evil people can become good. The Talmud tells the story of Rabbi Meir who was constantly harassed by a neighborhood bully. He used to pray that the bully would die. Then one day his wife Beruriah heard him and said he was mistaken. She told her husband, *Don't pray that he should die. Pray that he should change his ways.*"

Heather commented, "It sounded like she should have been the rabbi."

I answered, "Many think Beruriah should have been a rabbi. In a way she was a rabbi, if rabbi means *teacher*. Anyway, this is the perfect segue to what I want to teach today. If our tradition forbids us from hurting other people, what kind of sexual acts are hurtful? When does sex destroy the dignity of another human being?"

Heather spoke out. "Rape."

"Rape is one answer. Most people consider rape not sex at all, but an act of control and violence. Tell me, is it rape if a husband forces himself on his wife against her will?"

After a pause, Miriam answered. "If it is a marriage, isn't she obligated to satisfy his needs?"

I answered, "In Judaism it is the opposite. He is obligated to satisfy her needs. And even in a marriage, *no means no*. If she says no, he is forbidden to have his way with her."

Heather responded again. "Judaism sounds strangely liberal for a patriarchal religion."

"You would be surprised what Judaism teaches. But give me another example. Rape is obvious. When else is sex immoral?

This time my son actually spoke up. "Incest."

"Correct," I said. "Most of the forbidden sexual acts we read about on Yom Kippur deal with incest. A man and his father's wife, a man and his son's wife, etc. But can anyone think of an example of incest in the Bible where God looked the other way?"

I paused for a moment but nobody thought of the answer. "How about Lot and his daughters? After the destruction of Sodom and Gomorrah, Lot's two daughters thought that they were the last three people left on earth. It was their job to repopulate the world. So both of the two daughters got their father drunk, slept with him, got pregnant, and brought a new life into the world."

"Ooh, gross," said Miriam.

"God never condemned them. What other sexual activity?"

My son spoke again. "Adultery."

"Adultery is against the Ten Commandments. But tell me, if adultery is wrong, how was Abraham allowed to take the handmaiden Hagar?"

Shlomo spoke, "In those days a man could have more than one wife. I remember Rabbi Levovic telling us that it was Rabbeinu Gershom in the Middle Ages who finally outlawed polygamy."

"Correct. The answer is that in Biblical times, a woman could only have sexual relations with her husband. But a man could have more than one wife, a wife and a concubine, or like King David, even multiple wives and concubines. Why? Why was the Bible more concerned with the sexual behavior of women than men?"

Some of the students seem to gasp, uncomfortable with the clear sexism of the Bible. But Katy spoke up. "I know. With women, the Bible was worried about who the father is. If a woman could sleep with more than one man, then we are not sure of paternity."

"So what," I said. "Why is paternity important?"

Katy thought for a second. "If you don't know who the father is, then no man will take responsibility for the child. The Bible wants fathers to be around, to be present in their children's lives. And men being men, they want to know that the child is *theirs*."

Shlomo spoke up. "I was raised by a step-father who was more like a father to me than my own dad. You don't need to sire a child to be a father."

I replied, "True, there are plenty of step-dads, adoptive dads, foster dads who are wonderful fathers. But such fathers have made a deliberate decision to raise a child they did not sire. It takes a special man to do that. Too often men want to know the child is *theirs* before they commit to fatherhood. That is why paternity tests are so popular today.

"You always know who the mother is, but we want to know who the father is. We want fathers around to claim the child and help take care of him or her. In fact, if a woman has a baby with someone other than her husband, by Jewish law the child is tainted. We call such a child a *mamzer*. A *mamzer* has severe limitations in Jewish law, including who he or she can marry."

Heather shouted, "That's not fair."

"You are right, sometimes Jewish law is not fair."

Shmuel spoke up. "Who are you to say that Jewish law is unfair? It is God's law. God must have a reason for making a child into a *mamzer*. I will ask Rabbi Lebovic why a child of adultery is a *mamzer*."

I looked at him. "I am sure he will say the same thing, it is God's law. But some rabbis like myself believe that we need to make changes in God's law."

The hour was getting late, and there was one more topic I needed to cover. "Can anyone think of another example of sexual activity which is unethical? I paused for a moment, then spoke, "Suppose you get to college, and a professor gives you a poor grade, a grade you believe you do not deserve. Suppose the professor says he or she will change the grade if you have sex with them. Is that unethical?"

Katy gasped. "Does that really happen?"

"It absolutely happens. It could be your professor, or your boss, or your doctor, or some celebrity you adore. I believe sex is unethical whenever one partner has power over the other and uses that power to make sexual advances. I think sex is immoral between a teacher and a student, between a doctor and a patient, between a rabbi and a congregant, between a movie producer and a young actress. This kind of improper sexual behavior is too common. Sex should not be about power."

Heather spoke up again. "Too many men try to take advantage of women. It is like rape. I heard about those movie producers who would only give a young actress a part of she slept with him."

"You are right. But who is the first example in the Bible of a person who used their sexual power to try to seduce someone else?

It was actually a woman. Potaphar's wife tried to use her power to seduce the young Hebrew man in her house, Joseph. Joseph resisted her. When he refused her, she accused him of rape and had her husband send him to jail. But sex where one person has power over the other is wrong. I know rabbis who have lost their pulpits, or even rabbis in jail, for forgetting this."

"We will be looking at a variety of sexual activity in this class. It is as if there is a ladder of behavior, not just from evil to good but from unholy to holy. Certainly at the bottom of the ladder is sex that hurts another. We will be climbing that ladder of sexual behavior in this class." My time was up. "Have a good day."

Class was over. I felt that I had barely scratched the surface of unethical sex. And I was worried about David.

11. GOD PROTECTS THE INNOCENT

Rabbi Williams waited outside Dr. Baker's office. She had called this meeting, leaving a message at his synagogue that she wanted to meet with him as soon as possible. Rabbi Williams could not figure out why this woman made him so uncomfortable. He was a prominent rabbi of a large synagogue. She was the headmistress of a school where both his children attended. In a sense, he paid her salary. Yet when he was in her presence, he always felt like a student sent to the principal's office.

"Come in, Rabbi," she said. Her lack of a smile and curt style already put him off. As usual, there were no niceties, no small talk. She was all business. She shook his hand and said, "Please take a seat."

"Rabbi, I called you into my office because there are some concerns about your class. Some members of the school's board of trustees have already asked me to cancel it. They believe that your approach to sexuality is too liberal for a Jewish school. I will admit that I believe Rabbi Lebovic has been stirring things up."

Rabbi Williams was taken aback. "Too liberal, how so?"

"Some of the board members are blaming you and your class for what happened to David Eisenberg."

Now Rabbi Williams felt his ire rising. "Blame me! I have been David's rabbi since he was a little boy. I was the first one at the hospital when his parents called me. Tell me, a seventeen-year-old boy gets a fake ID, goes to a gay bar meant for patrons over twenty-one, then goes out into an empty parking lot late at night to call an Uber. On top of that, he is wearing a Jewish star. David is a wonderful young man, but it strikes me that he made a series of poor choices that night. Young people make poor choices. How can they possibly blame me or my class?"

Dr. Baker stared at him for a moment before responding. "Obviously you did not cause him to make those choices. But the feeling is that once you teach more liberal sexual ethics, students will test limits. Rabbi Lebovic claims that Jewish sexual ethics are very clear - black and white. Sex outside of marriage, gay sex, even masturbation are strictly forbidden. Even physical contact between boys and girls is forbidden. Only sex within marriage, between a man and woman, is permitted. He claims that this is what you should be teaching."

"Dr. Baker, with all due respect, Rabbi Lebovic represents a different world. It is not the world of these youngsters. It is not the world they see in their television shows and movies and rock videos. They see casual sex, sex without commitment. Boys and girls mingle together not just in school, but in the youth groups and at the mall. The casual attitude towards sex is what I am fighting. Most of my class will probably not be married until they are in their late twenties or early thirties, if they marry at all. Some like David are gay. If I tell them, no touching until you are married, they will laugh me right out of the classroom." Rabbi William's voice echoed against the office walls.

"Rabbi, please calm down. I am only reporting what is being said by some of the board of trustees. Tell me, last Monday in class, did you say that sex between teenagers is not immoral?"

"What?!" Rabbi Williams tried to remember what he taught in the last class that could have led to that opinion.

Dr. Baker looked at a piece of paper on her desk. "Here is what was reported to me. You spoke about a ladder of sexual behavior, from evil to good, from unholy to holy. Under evil you included adultery, rape, sexual harassment, but not what I consider the most important. You did not include sex between high school students as something on the bottom of the ladder. It may not be holy but it is not wrong either. Am I quoting you correctly?"

"Dr. Baker, I am not condoning teen sexual behavior. I would never do that." He wondered who had reported him to the headmistress, or more likely to parents who reported him to the headmistress. He thought about asking his students to be more discrete but realized that it was appropriate for them to discuss what he brought up in class with their parents.

"Rabbi, according to Rabbi Lebovic you perform gay weddings. Is that true?"

His jaw clenched as his voice shook with anger. "Whether or not I perform gay weddings is not your business, nor Rabbi Lebovic's business, nor the school's business. What I do ritually is up to my rabbinic organization, my own conscience, and God."

Dr. Baker took a deep breath. "Fair enough, rabbi. I will let you continue to teach the class. I will tell the board members of our school that we spoke. But I think you must make it explicit that we do not condone sexual activity between high school students. And let us pray for David's full recovery. Thank you, rabbi." She stood to shake his hand. If he had walked into her office nervous, he walked out furious. Rabbi Lebovic was not the only authority on Judaism at this school. And who was reporting to the headmistress what he taught in his class?

Isar Amir picked up his cheeseburger from the food court at the mall and started to walk back to his friend Joshua Williams. Then he saw Heather Hall sitting by herself. As usual, she had changed out of her school uniform and was now wearing a sexy, midriff-baring tank top, shorts, and sandals. She certainly caught the eye of many of the guys at the mall, and as Isar knew, she seemed to relish the attention.

Isar walked over and sat next to her.

"Aren't you sitting with Joshua?"

"He can wait. Heather, I had a thought. I want you to come to my home and do some tutoring for me."

Heather looked surprised. "Tutoring, in what subject?

You are better than me in both math and English."

"You know what subject."

Heather looked a bit embarrassed. "Has your friend Joshua been talking too much?"

"Heather, you knew he would talk. Is there a teenage boy in the world who will do it and not brag to his friends? I would like a tutoring lesson, like you gave Joshua. My parents are gone during the day. My home is empty."

"Sorry, Isar. I am not interested."

"I thought this is something you are doing for all the boys in our class. Your mitzvah project, so to speak."

"Isar, let me tell you what it means to be a mature woman. I tutor, to use your phrase, those who I choose to tutor. And I do not tutor, also to use your phrase, those who I choose not to tutor. My so-called mitzvah project is for those I choose. And I do not choose you. Now go back to your friend Joshua. Tell him he has a big mouth."

Isar knew it would take some convincing. "Listen Heather, in my family we pay tutors nicely. I will pay you."

Heather smiled. "Let me get this straight. You are willing to pay me to have sex with you. There is a name for that – prostitution. And it happens to be illegal."

"In the Bible, when Joshua conquered Jericho, he was helped by a prostitute named Rachav. She may have earned her living as a prostitute, but according to the rabbis she was a great heroine." Isar felt proud of himself that he knew that story. Only a Jewish day school student could quote a Biblical story to try to solicit a young woman for sex.

"And you are suggesting that I am a modern Rachav? A professional harlot." Heather enjoyed the back-and-forth banter.

"Yes."

"Isar. I do like you. Not as much as Joshua, but I do like you. But the Messiah will have to come before I agree to have sex with you."

"Heather, let me remind you of a conversation we had the first day of the Rabbi's sex class. You called that prostitute with the seven beds, six of silver and one of gold, a successful businesswoman. You complained how the woman had to shut down her business to become a rabbi's wife. You could be a successful businesswoman." He gestured towards her and then pointed to himself. "I can help you."

Heather smiled. "Isar, you're a pig."

"Think about it, we will speak further," he said as he walked away and went to join Joshua.

Nicolas arrived at Katy's house about 4 pm. She brought him into her kitchen and brought out a couple of cokes. "Don't worry," she said. "No one will bother us. My mom won't be home from work for at least two hours."

"I am sorry we can't go to my house. I am the oldest of six. There are always kids around. Besides, my parents are so overprotective, they look at everything I do. Anyway, I got them."

Nicolas opened up the box of condoms. "I was so nervous my hands were shaking. In fact, they are still shaking."

"How would your priest feel about you buying these?"

"He absolutely would not approve. But he might make me recite some *Our Fathers* or do the Rosary. My parents would kill me if they found out. They are stricter than any priest. They would ground me for a month."

"So why did you risk it?" Katy asked.

"You know what they say, it is easier to ask forgiveness than permission. I loved doing it with you. But if you get pregnant, we are in deep trouble. Birth control is wrong, but abortion is an absolute no-no. If you got pregnant, there would be no choice. I would have to marry you. And my parents would never approve."

"Because I am Jewish?"

"Because I am too young. And you are too young. And yes, because you are Jewish."

Katy felt a whiff of regret. The first time they had done it without protection. Could she already be pregnant? She did not feel like herself. But she was sure that the first time you do it, you cannot get pregnant. She vaguely remembered a rabbinic teaching she had learned from Rabbi Lebovic. *God protects the innocent.* How would Rabbi Lebovic feel about her having sex with a boy who used a condom? He would certainly condemn it, particularly if he knew the boy was Catholic. What about Rabbi Williams? He would be more understanding but probably also condemn it. She was willing to have sex with Nicolas, but she could not chance getting pregnant.

She tried to remember what Judaism says about using condoms. If for Jews it was wrong, for Catholics it was a mortal sin. Wasn't Nicolas worried about his soul?

"Nicolas, why does the Catholic Church totally outlaw birth control?"

He thought for a moment. "We studied that in our theology class. It goes back to one of our greatest teachers, St. Thomas Aquinas. Aquinas taught a doctrine of natural law. Actually, he claimed that it goes all the way back to Aristotle. Everything has a purpose, a reason it exists. Every creative thing from plants to animals to humans seek to fulfill its purpose. Aristotle taught that everything must act in accordance with its purpose, its very nature. Aquinas built on this idea. It is part of nature for sex to lead to babies. That is why God created sex. Any sexual activity which does not have the potential of leading to pregnancy is therefore immoral. It goes against nature. That is why Catholics forbid homosexuality, masturbation, and any kind of birth control. It interferes with nature, with the purpose of sex."

"Wow, we never studied that idea of natural law in our class. But I remember Aquinas being mentioned in a class we took in Jewish thought. It was a class on Maimonides. Aquinas called Maimonides *The Rabbi*. I guess he tried to put Judaism and Aristotle together. But I do not think that Maimonides ever spoke about natural law."

Nicolas continued, "We Catholics believe that we can learn right and wrong from nature. Birth control is unnatural; it artificially prevents pregnancy. If a couple wants to avoid getting pregnant, they have to use a rhythm method, timing sex each month to avoid a woman's fertile period."

"That sounds difficult. Contraception sounds much easier. I do not know what Maimonides would say about natural law. But I know my rabbi constantly says that we must move beyond nature. Nature is neither good or bad. We must transcend nature, even improve on nature. Judaism would permit birth control if it improves on nature. But I do believe that a condom raises another issue. Spilling of seed unnecessarily is wrong."

Katy continued, "In the Torah, Judah the son of Jacob had three sons. The oldest was named Er, and he married a girl named Tamar. But God became angry with Er, and he died without children. By Jewish law, if someone dies without children, the brother must marry the widow."

"Really?!" Nicolas was surprised.

"Really, it is right there in Deuteronomy. The brother Onan was supposed to raise children in the place of his dead brother. But it says that when Onan came unto Tamar, he spilled his seed upon the ground. God punished Onan also and put him to death. That is why we use the word *onanism* for spilling of seed. The story goes on about the relationship between Judah the father-in-law and Tamar the daughter-in-law. Judah gets Tamar pregnant. But that is why Judaism forbids condoms. Even in English we call the spilling of seed onanism. Judaism forbids onanism."

"Wow," said Nicolas. "So if we use a condom, I will be

breaking natural law and you will be sinning like Onan and Tamar. I guess the sin is on both of us."

"Nicolas, it would be a disaster if I got pregnant. As you said, it is easier to ask forgiveness than permission. Your priest and my rabbi may not approve, but I see no choice." She kissed him. And then they walked into her bedroom. After some fumbling the first time, they quickly learned how to use a condom.

12. SIXTH CLASS
NON-MARITAL SEX

That Monday I walked into class without my usual enthusiasm. I was still upset by the threats of Dr. Baker to cancel the class. But she was not the only one who held me responsible for the terrible events that happened to David Eisenberg just over two weeks ago. During the week I had received a letter from David's parents, long-time members of my synagogue. The letter disturbed me deeply.

The letter read in its entirety,

Dear Rabbi Williams,

This letter is to inform you that our family is resigning from the synagogue effective immediately. We are also pulling our son out of your Monday afternoon sex ethics class. We certainly cannot blame you directly for David being beaten up at a gay bar. We believe he used poor judgement and also broke the law. He is being grounded after school when he returns next week. But, rabbi, we also believe you used poor judgement in your teachings. You have fostered a permissive attitude towards sexual behavior by young people who are not yet ready to make such sexual decisions. In particular, we believe your acceptance of homosexuality directly influenced our son to purchase a fake ID and show up at that gay bar. There are reasons why our tradition forbids homosexuality. We can no longer support a synagogue where you serve as the rabbi.

Sincerely,

the Eisenbergs

Fifteen years of watching a young man grow up, officiating at his bar mitzvah, greeting him at religious services and in our youth group, suddenly thrown out the window. I did not make him gay. Perhaps God made him gay. And I certainly would never have encouraged him to go to that gay bar. It did not matter that I had rushed to the hospital to be with him and his parents late that Saturday night. I knew from experience that when life goes wrong, it is often easier to blame the rabbi than blame God. I also knew from experience that as liberal as most Jews are about gays, it was a different matter when their own children came out of the closet. I would call them and try to convince them to reconsider their decision, both regarding the synagogue and the class. But I knew it would probably not help.

My students seemed to be dealing with their own difficult issues. My son sat in the back with his friend Isar, joking around as usual. Then Heather Hall walked into the class, turned and stared at the two of them, and they both seemed to cringe in their seats. I knew Heather's reputation for being more outgoing and perhaps sexually active then most girls her age. Something had happened between her and the two boys, but I am sure I would never find out what. Katy had a smile on her face, and turned to watch her best friend Miriam walk in. But Miriam did not sit next to her. She grabbed a seat in the corner, again looking like she was ready to cry.

It was time to begin class. But I knew there was an issue I had to deal with first. "Good afternoon. Today I want to talk about Judaism and sex outside marriage. But first I want to squash a rumor that is out there. Some people are saying that I approve of sexual behavior between high school students. I never said that, and I would never say that.

"We have been dealing with the theme of achieving holiness by covering up. I asked the question of not uncovering yourself for someone else until you are ready and mature enough to handle a sexual relationship. And I believe that high school students are not yet ready nor mature enough to uncover themselves. I have said in the past, and I will say it again today. Keep yourself covered up."

Shmuel Stern's hand immediately shot up. "Rabbi, that is not what Rabbi Lebovic is saying. He gave a sermon in synagogue last Shabbat. He attacked you, not by name, but everybody knew he was talking about you. He said there is a rabbi in town who is teaching young people that sex outside marriage is ok, homosexuality is ok, even masturbation is ok. He said that these teaching are against *halakha* and undermine the integrity of the Jewish family. He gave a sermon about Isaac and Rebecca in the Bible, how Abimelech saw them *playing with each other*. According to the rabbi, they were not playing chess. They were acting as husband and wife, which the Torah permits. But he went on to emphasize that such *playing* by non-married couples, particularly teenagers, is utterly forbidden. Rabbi Lebovic said that the job of a rabbi is to build a fence around the Torah. He claims you are tearing down that fence."

I looked at him sharply. "Please tell Rabbi Lebovic that he is welcome to attend my class. Then he can decide if I am tearing down fences." I knew the rabbi would never attend a class I teach. Nor would he attend a service I lead. Not if women sat with men and participated in the service. It was not in keeping with his severe orthodoxy. I could only teach the Torah as I understand it.

"What does Judaism say about sex outside marriage? Today I want to share another story from the Talmud. But a caveat. The story is a bit sexist. Remember that the Talmud was written over 1500 years ago, and it was written by men who often talked about women. Let us set aside the sexism for one moment and see what the story can teach us.

Heather's hand immediately shot up. "Rabbi, why are you teaching us all this sexist crap?"

Shmuel reacted immediately, "Heather, can you stop with your feminist crap!"

Heather turned to him, "Because you attend a synagogue that treats women like chattel, don't bring your male chauvinism to our class!"

"More women come to my synagogue each Shabbat morning than ever come to Rabbi William's synagogue! Do they consider themselves chattel?"

"Ok, enough! We can argue about Judaism and feminism later. Let's read the story." I did raise my voice, but deep down I felt a certain pleasure that my students felt comfortable arguing with one another in my class.

I passed out a sheet with a section of Talmud on it. I could have studied the original Hebrew text, but I was more interested in the content. "Who wants to read?" Heather almost jumped out of her seat to volunteer.

"The Man with a Passion for a Woman
(Talmud *Sanhedrin* 75a)

Rav Yehuda says that Rav says: There was an incident involving a certain man who set his eyes upon a certain woman and passion rose in his heart, to the point that he became deathly ill. And they came and asked doctors what was to be done with him. And the doctors said: He will have no cure until she engages in sexual intercourse with him. The Sages said: Let him die, but she may not engage in sexual intercourse with him. The doctors said: She should at least stand naked before him. The Sages said: Let him die, but she may not stand naked before him. The doctors suggested: The woman should at least converse with him behind a fence in a secluded area.. The Sages insisted: Let him die, but she may not converse with him behind a fence.

Rabbi Ya'akov bar Idi and Rabbi Shmuel bar Naḥmani disagree about this issue. One of them says: The woman in question was a married woman, and the other one says: She was unmarried. Granted, according to the one who says that she was a married woman, the matter is properly understood. But according to the one who says that she was unmarried, what is the reason for all this opposition? Rav Pappa says: This is due to the potential harm to the family name. Rav Aḥa, son of Rav Ika, says: This is so that the daughters of Israel should not be promiscuous with regard to forbidden sexual relations.

But if the woman was unmarried, let the man marry her. His mind would not have been eased by marriage, in accordance with the statement of Rabbi Yitzḥak. As Rabbi Yitzḥak says: Since the day the Temple was destroyed, sexual pleasure was taken away from those who engage in permitted intercourse and given to transgressors, as it is stated: *Stolen waters are sweet, and bread eaten in secret is pleasant* (Proverbs 9:17)."

I could tell from the giggles that the class found the text entertaining. "Here we have an argument between the doctors and the rabbis on whether an unmarried man and an unmarried woman can have sex, in order to save the man's life."

"Why didn't they ask the woman what she thinks?" Heather responded.

"Good question. But in that day and age, the voices of women were often silenced. Let us not judge an ancient text by the standards of today." I continued, "The Talmud suggests that perhaps the woman is married, and that is why such sex is forbidden. It would be adultery. But then, the Talmud continues that she is single. So what is the problem? Let them have their sexual encounter to save his life? The text gives two reasons. But why do you think the Rabbis forbade it?"

Lewis spoke up. "If the Rabbis said yes, anybody could claim 'give me sex or I will die.' You spoke about sex as the evil inclination. If the Rabbis permitted this, it would be out of control."

"Lewis, you are on the right track," I responded. "I believe that if the Rabbis permitted this, then casual unmarried sex would become the norm. This is what the Rabbis were trying to prevent. If the young woman slept with the man, she would have difficulty finding a marriage partner later. Notice that the Torah does not say a man shall leave his father and mother for a series of one-night stands and casual hook-ups. It says a man shall leave his father and mother and cleave unto his wife. The Rabbis want to encourage marriage. So they outlawed casual sex, even to save a life. The Talmud continues the story, why does he not simply marry her? They answer that since the destruction of the Temple, people want sex in an illegitimate way. For as the book of Proverbs says, *Stolen waters are sweet.*"

Lewis continued, "I did not know there were so many stories about sex in the Talmud. It seems to be the only thing on the Rabbis' mind. My parents told me that when they were still Southern Baptists, nobody talked about sex. Certainly, no Baptist preacher would give a sermon about sex."

"Perhaps many Christians identify sex with sins of the flesh, something that one should avoid. That has never been the Jewish teaching. Judaism says that sex is something holy, with the right person at the right time. Casual, recreational sex falls short of that holiness ideal.'

Gary Brown spoke out, as I knew he probably would. "Rabbi, I disagree with everything you said. Darwin teaches the importance of genetic survival, of passing one's genes to the next generation. In fact, Richard Dawkins spoke about the selfish gene. I know he was an atheist, but I believe he was correct. Every creature tries to get his or her genes to survive. It is human nature for men to sleep around with as many sexual partners as they can. For a man to limit himself to one sexual partner is unnatural."

Heather spoke up, "Gary, let's see if you can find any sexual partners."

"Heather, enough." I responded, "Gary raises a good point. That is what male animals do, try to spread their seed around. But we humans are different from animals, at least according to Judaism. Our job is to rise above our nature."

At that moment the class ended. I am not sure I had convinced the class of anything.

13. SEX AND *KABBALAH*

Miriam hurried out of school. She planned to meet her friend Katy at the mall, the first time they would meet outside school in several weeks. She was aware that Katy was dating Nicolas, even if Katy's parents were clueless. Her parents, divorced but still hating one another, were caught up in their own lives and seemed to ignore Katy. Katy was happier than she had been for a long time, although her parents seemed to agree on only one thing: she should not be dating a non-Jew. They would never approve of Nicolas. Of course, Nicolas' parents would never approve of Katy either. Miriam thought that they sounded like a modern Romeo and Juliet. Two young people in love from two warring families. But this time it was not two families but two religions. She was concerned about what would happen to her friend.

As Miriam entered the student parking lot, she saw Kevin waiting. What was he doing here? She thought he was away at college. "Miriam, wait. Can we talk?" He stood between her and her car.

"Miriam, I drove down because I had to see you. I hate it

when you ignore my texts. I tried to call you. We had a good thing going. Miriam, I love you. I need you.."

Miriam stared at him. "Why did you keep pushing me to do what I did not want to do? Why did you refuse to erase the picture when I asked you to?"

"Miriam, I need that picture to see you when I am not with you. I love you. But I am a man. I have needs. All my friends in college have girls who help meet their needs. I was upset because you were holding out on me, not thinking about what I need. But I love you."

Miriam replied, "It sounds more like you love yourself."

"What do you mean?"

"Kevin, can I teach you something I learned from Rabbi Lebovic at the Hebrew Day School."

"Come on Miriam. I am not interested in all that Jewish stuff. Maybe I was in the youth group in high school, but in college I never go to the Hillel. Occasionally I have gone to Chabad, because they give a free Friday night dinner and all the booze you can drink. Sometimes I think students get more drunk at Chabad than at the fraternities. But don't lay all that Jewish stuff on me. I don't care about it."

"Kevin, my dad is president of the synagogue, I go to a Jewish day school, and this Jewish stuff is important to me. The rabbi shared with us the Jewish view of love."

"There is a Jewish view of love?" Kevin honestly looked surprised. "I thought Judaism is a religion of law, not of love."

"There is a Jewish view of love. The rabbis say there are two kinds of love. There is love dependent on something, conditional love, love where you want something. The example is the love in the Bible of Amnon and Tamar."

"Sorry, but I do not remember much Bible."

"Amnon and Tamar were half brother and sister, children of King David with different mothers. Amnon told Tamar how much he loved her. He wanted sex with her. Tamar said it was forbidden, so he forced himself on her. He raped her. And then he hated her. Out of this story a war broke out among David's children and Amnon was killed. The rabbis say this is conditional love, love where someone is out to get something. That love never lasts."

"Are you comparing my love for you to that of a rapist towards his own sister? Come on Miriam."

"I am not saying you are Amnon. But your love for me seems conditional. The rabbis go on to speak of unconditional love. It is love of two people, who love each other with no expectations. The rabbis say that is the love between King David and his best friend, King Saul's son Jonathan. Jonathan sacrificed his kingship to save David's life. David said his love for Jonathan is more than the love of a woman."

"It sounds like they were queer. Do you want me to love you like two queer men?"

Miriam looked at him in disgust. "I think we need to take some time apart. Now get out of my way." She pushed him aside as she got into her car and drove to the mall. She would be late to meet her friend Katy.

Katy's face had a shine these past weeks. Miriam could not remember her best friend being this happy. Miriam was both happy for her and worried. Eventually she will be forced to tell her parents about Nicolas. Who knows how they would react. She felt bad being late, but Katy was sitting in the food court sipping a rich drink from Starbucks. She stood up and gave Miriam a hug.

"Sorry I am late. Guess who confronted me in the parking lot of the school." Katy looked at her concerned. "Kevin. He drove down from college to see me."

"Are you two back together?"

"I am afraid we had words. I broke up with him. He is a pig. I think I knew that all along, but I was too enamored with dating a college guy to notice. It is over." Miriam forced a smile but looked like she was ready to cry.

Katy took her hand sympathetically. "Miriam, you are the prettiest, nicest girl in the entire senior class. Probably in the entire school. There are guys who would give anything to have you as a girlfriend. You do not need him. Good riddance."

"Thanks, Katy. What about you? It has been too long since we have gotten together outside of school. Do your parents know about Nicolas?"

"Not yet. I don't know what do. I love him and I believe he loves me. We sometimes talk for hours."

"What do you talk about for hours?"

"Mostly religion. He is a very religious Catholic. Goes to church each Sunday, confession once a month. In fact, he has an uncle who is a priest. His parents practice that no birth control teaching. He is the oldest of six children."

Katy continued. "We talk a lot about religion. He speaks about being Catholic and I speak about being Jewish. It is almost like I have more in common with him than most the boys in our Jewish school. They talk about sports and video games and how they cannot wait to leave their parents and go off to college. He talks about his parents and family and how close they are. I guess, with divorced parents and no brothers or sisters, I miss not having a family."

Katy leaned closer to her. "Miriam, can I tell you something? We often meet in my home when my mother is at work. We have been sleeping together. At first it was really awkward. But now I look forward to it. He has learned how to make me feel good. I know what the rabbi said in class – high school students are too young. But we are seniors. And we truly love each other. If we love each other, how can it be a bad thing?"

Miriam was taken aback. She did not expect this. She felt a twinge of jealousy pass through her. She knew she was the pretty one. Now her friend Katy, not as pretty nor as popular as her, had lost her virginity first. Her friend was sexually active, while she had broken up with her boyfriend because he wanted sex. Maybe it was a mistake to break up.

"Katy, I am happy for you. I truly am. I hope you two are

being careful."

"Yes, we always use a condom."

"I thought it was against Catholic law to use birth control."

"Nicolas says he would rather ask for forgiveness than for permission. Besides, I think he makes confession to his priest."

"He tells his priest about your sexual life?" Miriam thought about Nicolas discussing this with his priest. Could she ever discuss with a clergy such a private matter? Then she remembered telling Rabbi Williams about posing nude for Kevin. She was embarrassed. What did the rabbi say? Keep herself covered up. Do not uncover for anyone until you are absolutely sure it is the right person. And tell Kevin to destroy the picture. Of course, Kevin had refused. He was a pig. Miriam wished she could find a nice guy like Nicolas.

Katy continued. "I don't care what he tells his priest. We always use a condom. The only time we did not was the first time we had sex."

"Katy, why not?"

"Someone told me that the first time a woman has sex, she cannot get pregnant."

"Katy, who told you that? It is not true. You can get pregnant every time you have sex. All it takes is one sperm reaching one egg. Please don't do that again."

Katy's face fell as a sense of dread overtook her.

Joshua and Isar went to Rabbi Lebovic's Orthodox synagogue that Shabbat. It was the *yahrzeit* of Isar's grandfather, and his father wanted to say *kaddish*. He found someone to cover his booth at the flea market and convinced the boys to go along with him. Joshua did not love the synagogue. Services were even longer than his father's, with less singing and more mumbling in Hebrew. But worse, the girls were all hidden behind a high partition. His classmate Shmuel said there were a lot of girls there. But what good was it if he could not see them.

Then he thought, even if I meet a girl here, she is not likely to treat me as Heather had. Following the night in the hotel room with Heather, he thought about how to have a second experience. But it was unlikely to happen anytime soon. His thought wandered as the prayers went on around him, although he noticed how Isar stood up when his father was called to the Torah. It was a sign of respect. He also noticed how Isar's father pledged $100 to the synagogue.

He listened as Rabbi Lebovic got up to deliver his sermon. He was a good speaker. Joshua wondered if he would continue the theme of a few weeks ago, of Abimelech seeing Isaac and Rebecca *playing* in their bedroom. He was not disappointed.

"*Gut Shabbes*. Welcome. Today I want to talk about something that is strange, and occasionally beautiful. I am speaking of the Jewish mystical tradition of *kabbalah*. I know that the Talmud warns against studying kabbalah, and some sources limit it to males over forty who are deeply learned. But today, since everybody, even Madonna, claims to be a kabbalist, I want to share a bit of authentic *kabbalah*. I have never been much of a kabbalist, the yeshiva where

I learned prefers studying *halakha* or Jewish law to *kabbalah* or Jewish mysticism. But let us learn together.

"We always say in Judaism that God is One. But in *kabbalah* the idea is more complex. The oneness of God is broken. There are masculine aspects of God and feminine aspects of God, or as a kabbalist might put it, masculine *sefirot* and feminine *sefirot*. The *sefirot* are the ten manifestations of God in the created universe. The masculine aspects of God are called *Teferes*." Joshua cringed a bit at the old Ashkenazic pronunciation. His dad sometimes talked about this. He called it *Teferet*, as they would in modern Israel. "The feminine aspects of God are called *Shekhinah* – God's indwelling in the world. And according to *kabbalah*, *Teferes* and *Shekhinah* have become separated. It is almost as if God has become divided. And here is the great insight. Our job, as pious Jews, is to put God back together again. In fact, before many mitzvot, kabbalists literally say a formula that begins, 'I do this mitzvah to reunite the Holy One with His *Shekhinah*.'"

"The role of the Jew is to reunite what has been broken. There is a fancy word which scholars use for our actions that help God – theurgy." Joshua tried to secretly look at his cell phone and find a definition of theurgy. The use of electronic devices is forbidden on the Jewish Sabbath, so he hid it under his jacket to look. The definition popped up. Theurgy is when human actions affect the divine. How did Rabbi Lebovic know such a fancy word? "Here is the great insight of *kabbalah*. When a husband and wife come together with the correct intention and attitude, particularly on the Sabbath evening, their act has cosmic consequences. The marital act is helping to reunite *Teferes* and *Shekhinah*, God's masculine and feminine aspects. Our actions in the lower world can affect what happens in the higher world. That is why Judaism considers the marital bed to be a place of holiness, and the marital act to be holy."

After this lesson in *kabbalah*, Rabbi Lebovic switched gears. "However, there is a problem in the Jewish community. There are people who call themselves rabbis who deny the holiness of the marital bed, the holiness of the relationship between a husband and a wife. There are those that claim that sexual activity between any two people – married or unmarried, a man and a woman or two men or two women, is okay. This attitude makes sure that God stays broken. Such people undermine the holiness of the act." Joshua knew exactly whom the rabbi was speaking about. He thought about his father and did not tune into the rest of the sermon.

When services were over, Isar held up something to show Joshua. "Look what I have. Two tickets to The New Dead. It is a Grateful Dead tribute band. When you listen to them, you will think that Jerry Garcia was resurrected and brought back to life. We are going. The tickets are for a week from Friday night. At least we will have something exciting to do during winter break."

Joshua was taken aback. "I don't know if I can. My parents want me home for Shabbat dinner. Besides, that Friday night we are having the Pollacks over. He is president of my dad's synagogue. Miriam will be there. They are returning home from vacation."

"If the rabbi can speak of pleasure on Friday night, you and I can find our own pleasure Friday night." Joshua knew that an argument was coming. But he would approach his parents. He had no way of knowing that the Pollacks would cancel, for reasons that would surprise the entire senior class.

14. SEVENTH CLASS
CLIMBING THE LADDER

The moment I began the class, Shmuel spoke out. "Did you hear that Rabbi Lebovic attacked you during his sermon on Shabbat?"

"So I heard." I did not want the class to know that my son had been in Rabbi Lebovic's synagogue and afterwards told me the whole story. As it was, Joshua looked a bit embarrassed.

Shmuel continued, "Is the Rabbi right? Do you really believe it is ok for unmarried people to have sex?" To Shmuel, Rabbi Lebovic was *the Rabbi*. I was just one of his teachers, not a real rabbi.

I asked the class, "When we spoke about the young man who would die if he did not have sex with a particular young woman, and the rabbis said, 'Let him die,' did I sound like someone who condones non-marital sex?"

"So you think that only married couples should be allowed to have sex?" Shmuel was persistent.

"I didn't say that either. What I oppose is casual, recreational sex. What young people often call hook-ups. Two young people meet at a bar, go home together, and hop into bed. Sometimes they do not even know each other's names. Maybe they treat each other very nicely, maybe they practice safe sex, doing what is necessary to avoid pregnancy or sexually transmitted diseases. But then they go their separate ways, possibly not to see each other again.

"I will not say this activity is unethical. They treated one another with respect. I imagine they are two very nice young people. But I do believe that it falls far short of the Jewish vision of holiness that we spoke about. And I believe it is a disincentive to marriage. Let me ask you a question. Let us suppose that you went online and found someone you would consider the perfect marriage partner. They have all the values you are looking for. But suppose, in a candid moment, they admit that they have had thirty other sexual partners in the past year. Now that they met you, they would be faithful. Would you be comfortable with that relationship?"

Katy spoke, "I don't know if I would be comfortable. Could I trust them to go from thirty to one partner suddenly."

Heather responded, "I don't agree. I would want a marriage partner who is experienced. Someone who knows what they are doing."

Isar called out, "So teach me!"

I gave him a sharp look and responded to Heather, "I suppose there is a world of difference between someone experienced and someone promiscuous."

Shmuel immediately jumped on my words. "So you do believe someone should marry a person who is experienced. It looks like Rabbi Lebovic is correct. You do condone sex outside of marriage."

"Let me say a bit more. Rabbi Lebovic lives in a world where people marry very young, probably around eighteen. Boys and girls do not mingle. When they reach the age of marriage, introductions are arranged, sometimes by parents and sometimes by a professional matchmaker, a *shadchan*. They meet in a public place, a hotel lobby or park or museum, and talk. They often meet several times. If they are compatible, the wedding is arranged fairly quickly. They are never alone together until the wedding night. It is a way to control the sexual desire of young people. And it works, at least for that community, at least most of the time. Sometimes disastrous marriages result."

"In the community I serve, young people want to go to college, to receive professional degrees, establish themselves in careers, date other people. They often do not get married until well-into their thirties."

"If they get married at all," Heather replied.

"Correct, if they get married at all. The question is, do I really expect people to avoid all sexual activity until their thirties or later. I do not believe that is realistic. The Talmud says that when we get to the next world, we must give an account for every legitimate pleasure we did not enjoy. Sex is a legitimate pleasure in

Judaism. I understand that young people today will be sexually active."

"So you do condone sex outside of marriage." Shmuel seemed obsessed with my thoughts on the subject.

"I suppose I do. If it is between two people who are older than high school age, two people in love, two people in an exclusive relationship, two people who are contemplating marriage, two people who treat each other decently. In fact, I think that sometimes such pre-marital sex might be healthy. It can be terrible when two people get married and only then discover they are sexually incompatible. I believe such sex must be in the context of a relationship, a relationship where they truly seek *to know* one another. Remember, *to know* is the Biblical term for sex.

"In an earlier class I spoke of a ladder of holiness regarding sexual behavior. At the bottom of the ladder is sex that destroys, hurtful sex. Higher up the ladder is casual, recreational sex, the two people who pick up one another in a bar but do not know each other. Higher up is sex within the context of a relationship, two people who have made a commitment to one another. Hopefully this will lead to marriage. And we will be talking about the top of the ladder, sex within marriage. But my goal is to see people climbing this ladder, which I call *the ladder of holiness*."

Shmuel was not finished. "What happens when these two people in love, perhaps planning to get married someday, discover that the woman is pregnant. Aren't you advocating having children outside marriage?"

How quickly he had changed the subject. "I do not advocate having children outside marriage, although it sometimes happens. I believe children need a mother and father who are present in their lives, and marriage is the traditional way to make sure they are both present. Being a single parent is tough." I noticed that Katy winced at my words. "That is why I believe an unmarried couple who are sexually active should practice birth control."

Suddenly Lewis spoke up, "I thought Jews do not believe in birth control."

"The issue of birth control is complex. But we are not Catholics." Again, I saw Katy cringe. I sensed this class was making her uncomfortable. "Most Jewish authorities permit birth control by women. By Jewish law, she is not obligated to be fruitful and multiply. Most Jewish authorities forbid it by men, because of the spilling of seed. Remember the story of Onan and Tamar in the Bible. He spilled his seed rather than have children in the name of his dead brother. Traditional Jewish law forbids condoms. But some authorities say, if there is an overwhelming reason such as health, even condoms are permitted."

Heather spoke out again, "Do you think our school should be giving out condoms to students?"

I smiled. "Several of you are challenging me on everything today. No, I do not believe the school should be giving out condoms to teens. It would be seen as permission to become sexually active. But I believe condoms are permissible. And people who are sexually active outside of marriage should use them.

"I would rather see birth control then abortion. I would rather stop a pregnancy before the fact than terminate after the fact. These are complex issues and I am afraid we have run out of time today. After winter break we move to the top of the ladder – sex within marriage." I looked again at Katy. Something was bothering her. I would find out soon enough.

During the winter break (Eastman Jewish Academy would not use the words *Christmas break*), several of my students would be traveling. I knew that the Pollacks would be going on a skiing trip to Colorado. Shmuel Stern's family was going to Chicago to visit relatives, but Shmuel asked to stay behind. His relatives in Chicago were not kosher nor did they observe the Sabbath. But Shmuel's parents were forcing him to go.

As for my family, we never travelled over the winter break. I had services to conduct, and Hanukkah was coming. Although a relatively minor holiday in the Jewish calendar, it was a major celebration for members of my synagogue. They wanted their rabbi present. My family vacations were brief and usually occurred during the summer. But lately Joshua and Shira both felt too old to travel with Marcia and me.

I would use the winter break to plan my next class. How would I explain the marital bedroom to these young people, who were probably a decade or two from getting married?

15. THE CONCERT

It was the first day of winter break and Miriam was packing for the family ski trip. They would leave tomorrow morning for the airport. Unlike many of her friends, she still enjoyed traveling with her parents. And she loved skiing. Her parents were downstairs eating breakfast, and her brother Eddie was not home, sleeping at a friend's house. But she wanted to get an early start packing.

Then her friend Katy called. "Look at your phone. Open your Instagram account."

"What is it?"

"Just look," Katy said.

She opened the account and gave a scream. She screamed again and threw her phone across the room. Her parents came running up the stairs. The screams were like something from a horror movie. Then she laid across her bed sobbing.

Her mom Susan was the first to speak. "Honey, what's wrong?" But Miriam would not speak. She simply kept crying. Susan sat next to her and put her arms around her, trying to comfort her. But the sobs were interminable. Barry walked across the room to where Miriam had thrown the cell phone. He picked it up and looked. And to his horror, he realized why his daughter had screamed and why she was crying.

The phone was open to her Instagram account. And there was a picture of their daughter, sitting on her bed, as naked as the day she was born. Everybody could see her. And everybody had. There were comments, comments from people she knew in school and comments from strangers. Tens of comments, and they kept coming. Some were comforting, "Miriam, call me." Some were accusing, "Miriam, how can you do this?" And some, particularly from the boys, were rude and heartless. "You're hot, baby." "I need you." Barry shut the phone and sat next to his daughter who was now whimpering.

"Who did this, Miriam? Who did this to you?"

With her parents on either side of her and Susan's arm around her, Miriam was finally able to talk. "Katy just called me. She told me to open my Instagram account. I opened it and there was the picture. Already there were hundreds of views. Kevin put it up there."

Barry's face was turning red. "Kevin did this! Miriam, who took this picture? Did Kevin sneak a picture when you were not looking? How did he get this picture?"

Susan hugged her daughter more tightly. Miriam spoke softly, "He did not take the picture. He was not even here. I took the picture. It is a selfie. I took it and I sent it to him."

"Miriam, you took this. But why? Why would you do such a thing?"

"I don't know, Dad. He asked me to. He kept saying he loves me. He needs me. He misses me. If we could not see each other in person, at least he could look at me. I guess I was lonely, too. So I sent the picture. The minute I did it, I regretted it. I asked him to erase it, but he refused. He said it makes him happy when he looks at it."

Susan knew that she had to comfort her daughter while soothing her husband's anger. She spoke, trying to keep her voice calm. "So why did he do this, send a private picture out for everyone to see?

"Mom, it was his way of getting even with me. I broke up with him. He kept pushing me for sex and I refused. He said the meanest things to me. Finally, I had enough, and told him we should spend some time apart. Dad, Mom, I am so sorry. Please forgive me." Then she started sobbing again.

Barry and Susan waited for the sobbing to subside. Then Barry spoke softly to her, "Sweetie, let me call my law office and see if there is any legal action we can take against him. What he did is probably criminal."

Miriam started sobbing again. Her mom held her and said to her husband, "Barry, I think we ought to postpone the skiing trip. There are more important issues to deal with."

Barry spoke softly to his daughter. "Did anyone know about this before today?"

Miriam whimpered, "No one but me and Kevin. I told Katy but told her not to tell anyone. No one else. Except Rabbi Williams."

Barry suddenly exploded. "Rabbi Williams! Our rabbi knew that our daughter had posed for a nude picture. And he did not tell us. Maybe we could have stopped it."

"I told the rabbi not to tell you. I made him promise. He said that as a rabbi he has a professional obligation not to share personal information with anyone. The only exception is if someone wants to harm themselves or others."

"And you do not think that Kevin wanted to harm you? The rabbi should have told us."

"I told the rabbi not to tell. He promised he would not tell. It is my fault. I took the selfie. I sent it to Kevin. I am to blame." Then she started weeping again. "Mom and Dad, I cannot go back to that school after this. What am I going to do?"

Her mom hugged her. Her dad said, "Let me make some phone calls, and see what I can do." Then he ran downstairs.

Barry first called his law partner and told him the entire story. "What can we do? Can we take legal action?" His partner asked for a little time to do some research.

One hour later his partner called back. "We are lucky. Our state has a law forbidding the distribution of sexually explicit material without permission. It is called *revenge porn*." Barry winced at the term *porn*. "Criminal charges can be brought against your daughter's boyfriend – or should I say, ex-boyfriend. We can also bring a civil suit. If it works in our favor, he could be in deep trouble. But it may be a tough fight. She gave him the picture willingly. He could claim that she consented. In a court of law, it would be his word against hers. And whether criminal or civil or both, it could drag on for years.

"There is something known as the Cyber Civil Rights Initiative. It is an organization that works with Facebook, Twitter, Instagram, and other social media sites to get them to remove such cyberporn. They recommend that you keep a copy of all the material and comments you find."

Barry was dumfounded. "Do you mean that I have to keep copies of nude pictures of my seventeen-year-old daughter? And all the horrid comments people made, the lewd reactions by her classmates and others. I have to save them all?"

"That is exactly what I mean. If we go to court you will need evidence. Do you want me to call the police?"

"Let me discuss it with my daughter. But first, let me call the rabbi."

When Rabbi Williams picked up the phone, Barry was fuming. "Rabbi, you knew my daughter posed for a nude picture and sent it to her boyfriend. And you chose not to tell us. She is a minor. It was your obligation to inform the parents."

Rabbi Williams took a deep breath. He knew the statement in the Talmud, one should not try to appease one's fellow at the height of their anger. "Barry, I cannot tell you whether I met with your daughter or not, whether I knew about this or not. If your daughter shared something with me, she shared it in confidence. Unless someone is planning to harm themselves or others, I have professional obligations regarding confidentiality."

"Someone was harmed! My daughter!"

"Barry, again I cannot share with you whether or not I met with your daughter and whether I knew anything. If something was said to me, it was said in confidence. I have professional obligations as a rabbi."

"Cut the bullshit, rabbi. I have obligations as a father. And you have obligations to me, as my rabbi. I am president of this synagogue, and your boss. Why did you not tell me about the nude photo?"

"Barry, I will talk to you calmly and I need you to listen. You are a very successful attorney. You know about attorney-client privilege. If a client told you something and you shared it with someone else, even their parents, what would happen to you? You know what would happen. You would be brought up on charges – probably disbarred. You have professional obligations. And as a rabbi, I also have professional obligations. Even if I met with your daughter, and I cannot tell you whether I did or not, I would not share anything without her permission."

Rabbi Williams continued, "Your anger should be against the boy who did this. I know Kevin; he grew up in my synagogue. Let me call him and see what I can do to get him to remove the picture."

Barry was not mollified, but deep down he knew the rabbi was right. "Call him. But tell Marcia that we will not be coming to dinner at your home next week. I will be lucky if I can ever get Miriam into synagogue again." Then Barry slammed the phone down.

It took three days and five phone messages before Kevin finally returned Rabbi William's call. He knew why Kevin was avoiding him. "Boy are you hard to reach."

Kevin sounded almost like he was crying. "Rabbi, I am so sorry. I know what I did was wrong. I did it because I was so angry at Miriam. I felt she was leading me on. The minute I uploaded that picture to my friends on Instagram, I regretted it. But it was too late. I am sorry. What can I do to make it up to her?"

The rabbi responded. "Kevin, I have known you for over a decade. We are all human and we do the wrong thing. But what you did was really hurtful. I do not think an apology is enough. Let me share a story with you. It is a classic story from Jewish tradition.

"Once there was a woman in a small town who spread evil gossip about the rabbi. Afterwards, she felt horrible. She came to the rabbi, asked for forgiveness, and asked what she could do. The rabbi told her he would forgive her, but first she must bring him a feather pillow. The woman was confused but did what the rabbi said. She handed him the pillow and said, *now am I forgiven*? Not yet, said the rabbi. *I want you to cut the pillow open, go outside, and scatter the feathers to the wind.* Again, the woman was confused, but did what the rabbi said. She watched the feathers blow off in every direction. *Now am I forgiven? Not yet*, said the rabbi. *One more thing. I want you to gather all the feathers up again. But that's impossible*, said the woman. *That's right. That is the trouble with gossip; once it is out there, you can never gather it up again.*"

Rabbi Williams continued, "What was true for gossip in the old country is even more true on social media. Once it is out there, you cannot gather it back in. I want you to take down as many copies of that picture as you can. But you know the picture will be out there forever."

Kevin still seemed to be crying, "How can I face Miriam again?"

The rabbi answered, "Do what you can to make this right. Take down the picture. Then apologize, not just to Miriam but to her parents. Maybe over time, they will see fit to forgive you. You really hurt her. I know you are better than that. Kevin, be a better person."

"I will. Rabbi, can I ask you something? I am not the most religious person, but I always go to synagogue on the High Holidays. My mom tells me that I will no longer be welcome in your synagogue on the holidays. That what I did was so wrong, I would be turned away."

"Kevin, you will not be turned away. On Yom Kippur, as we begin *kol nidre* services, on the holiest night of the year, the prayers say that we have permission to pray with people who sinned. Not only do we have permission, but even the worst sinner cannot be turned away on Yom Kippur. You are certainly not the worst sinner. But you wronged somebody. Now, try to make it right."

"I will, rabbi."

Rabbi Williams hung up, but he felt a deep sense of foreboding.

Katy sat in the car outside Nicolas' home. It was beautifully decorated with Christmas lights. Her home had a single Hanukkah *menorah* in the window. Katy knew she was not allowed in, so she waited for Nicolas to walk out to her. She had told Nicolas it was important, to meet her in the car. Nicolas had a driver's license, but his parents did not allow him to own a car. They told him that he could get one when he was eighteen. Katy's father had bought her a used car.

When Nicolas finally walked out to meet her, she was crying softly. "Sorry, I did not want my mom to see where I was going." Then he saw her crying. "What is the matter, Katy?"

Katy did not say anything but pulled a little white tube out of a bag. She showed him and he looked puzzled. "What's that."

"Nicolas, it's a pregnancy test. Look, see the plus signs? It shows I am pregnant."

"Are you sure?"

"I took three of them. Each one came out positive. My period was always regular. But now I am more than two weeks' overdue. And I just feel it. My breasts feel different, almost like a tingling. Something has changed in my body. I have not been to a doctor yet, but I know I am pregnant."

"But we have been using condoms."

"Not the first time we had sex."

"I thought you said that you can't get pregnant the first time."

Katy sniffled, "I was so wrong. Nicolas, what are we going to do? I cannot tell my parents; you cannot tell your parents."

Nicolas put his arm around her and pulled her close. He loved snuggling up to her. "Katy, we will have to be brave. We'll go together. First we'll tell your parents, then we'll tell my parents. We can't hide this. We can be there for each other. I love you. When we graduate high school next summer, we will both be eighteen. We will get married and raise the baby together. Everything will turn out all right."

Katy sobbed softly. "I can't. I can't have a baby now. I can't get married. My parents would kill me. I plan to go to college, to have a career. Someday I will have children. Not now. I can't. I need to make it go away."

"What do you mean?" Nicolas felt sick.

"I want to have an abortion. Would you help me get an abortion?"

He paused and stared at her. "Katy, it is absolutely forbidden. It is murder. You are talking about taking a human life. You cannot. I want to marry you and be a good father to this baby."

"I want to terminate this pregnancy. I do not want to have a baby now."

"Katy, come with me to talk to the priest. He will tell you it is forbidden, and why."

She looked at him. "Nicolas, you are a good Catholic, and you are speaking like a good Catholic. I am a good Jew. I need to turn to my own religion. I do not want to talk to a priest. Let me talk to my rabbi."

"I am sure the rabbi would say the same thing. Abortion is wrong. The Bible says so."

"Nicolas, I am going to speak with Rabbi Williams. He told us we could speak to him confidentially about anything. He would not tell our parents. When school starts, the first Monday after class I will meet with him. Perhaps he can tell me what to do."

Just then, Nicolas heard his mother's voice. "I've got to go. Talk to the rabbi. If you want, I can come with you."

"You're sweet, Nicolas. But no. I have to do this alone."

"Promise me you will not do anything drastic. And please don't kill our baby." Nicolas gave her a kiss and left her sobbing softly in the car.

It was the last Friday evening of winter break. Joshua and Isar waited at Joshua's home for the Uber. They would go downtown, and then return to Isar's home after the concert. That way Joshua would not disturb his parents; Joshua's dad had to be in synagogue both that evening and the next morning. Rabbi Williams, already dressed to go to synagogue, spoke to the two young men. "You know that I do not approve of you going to a rock concert on

Friday night. But I will not stop you. You need to make your own choices. However, I would like you to hear the Friday night *kiddush*."

Joshua and Isar put on yarmulkes as Rabbi Williams took a cup of wine to chant the blessing. He sipped, and Joshua and Isar also took a sip. He then put his hands on Joshua's head and blessed him, as he had done every Friday night since Joshua was born. He used the traditional words from the book of Genesis:

יְשִׂמְךָ אֱלֹהִים כְּאֶפְרַיִם וְכִמְנַשֶּׁה

"May God bless you as he blessed Efraim and Manasseh" (Genesis 48:20).

He referred to the two sons of Joseph, the first two boys in the Bible to get along.

A horn sounded. The Uber had arrived.

When Joshua and Isar arrived at the downtown venue, before standing in line to go through security, Isar handed Joshua a cigarette. "I don't smoke," he replied.

"You don't go to rock concerts on Friday night, either. There has to be a first time for everything." Isar lit a cigarette and handed it to Joshua. Joshua inhaled the tobacco smoke and immediately starting choking. Isar started laughing, and said, "You'll get used to it. Inhale slowly."

As Joshua nursed the cigarette, slowly getting used to the tobacco taste, Isar pulled something out of his pocket. "I have something else for you. Actually, two things." He handed Joshua a large white pill in a small envelope.

"What is this?" Joshua asked.

"Don't ask questions. I want you to swallow this pill when the concert begins. It will make you enjoy it more."

"Is it a drug? I don't take drugs."

Isar looked at the cigarette in Joshua's hand. "You don't smoke either. Just trust me. Take it. You will enjoy the concert. I have one more thing for you."

"What is that?" Isar handed Joshua a condom. "I don't need that."

"Just hold onto it. You might get lucky."

Joshua put it in his pocket, snuffed out the cigarette, and the two of them stood at the end of the long security line. Their excitement was building.

There was an opening band that was alright, but Isar said to wait before taking the pill. It was almost nine when the New Dead came out. Jerry Garcia had died several years before Joshua was born, but he had seen pictures of the founder of the Grateful Dead. Now he looked at the lead guitarist of the New Dead. If he did not know better, he could have passed for Jerry Garcia. Joshua swallowed the pill as the music began.

Joshua loved the music. Within a short time, he realized the pill was affecting him. It was as if his soul was separating from his body, floating up with the music. He remembered how his dad used to speak about Hasidic men who used ecstatic song and dance during prayer. His dad spoke about how their souls seem to separate from their bodies and commune with a higher power. He knew that such spiritual experiences never happened in his dad's placid synagogue. Now he was beginning to understand what his dad meant. He was leaving his body behind and becoming at one with the music. Although they had seats, nobody was sitting. Everyone was standing, swaying, moving to the music. He was not the only one who had taken drugs before the concert.

He felt the music. But he was also aware of blond curls that kept drifting into his line of sight. The curls swayed to the music. Only at midnight, the city's curfew for music venues, did he notice who the curls belong to. She was cute, with a slight figure and a sweet smile, a few years older than Joshua. She turned to him.

"My parents used to go to Grateful Dead concerts. I grew up listening to their music. What about you?"

Joshua thought about his parents. They had gone to a few concerts of Jewish music, Craig Taubman and Rick Recht. He remembered them going once to a Neil Diamond concert, and although they did not listen to country music, they once went to hear Dolly Parton. But he could not imagine his parents at a Grateful Dead concert, or any other rock band or jam band. "My parents never played this kind of music."

"Then let me introduce you to some Grateful Dead music. Not a tribute band but the real thing. I have it downloaded on my phone. Do you want to go somewhere and listen?"

"I think my friend wants to go home." But Isar looked at him and shrugged, as if to say, *you got lucky. I will be fine.*

She continued, "You can call me Susy."

"Hi, I'm Joshua."

"Listen Joshua, there is a hotel next door that is not too expensive." She took his arm to walk towards the exit. He waved goodbye to Isar. "Do you have some cash on you?"

"Not a lot. But I have a debit card."

"Good. Get a room and we will listen to music." They walked to a hotel across the street. "I am going to the restroom. You get us a room." Joshua went to the desk and was taken aback. *Not too expensive* was more than $200. But he liked her blond curls, loved her smile, and thought, *why not.* Joshua paid for the room.

The room was small, a queen bed, dresser, television, and desk. Joshua and Susy sat on the bed listening to the Grateful Dead on her phone. Joshua still felt the effects of the pill he had taken. Before long they were kissing. She undressed him and then took off her clothes. Joshua took out the condom but fumbled with it. "Let me help you." She was obviously more experienced than him, and he decided to let her take the lead. Soon they were in bed. And for the second time in as many months, Joshua experienced the pleasure of sex.

Joshua awoke the next morning feeling the aftereffects of a busy night. What time was it? He felt woozy. He looked for Susy in the bed next to him, but she was not there. *Perhaps she is in the shower*, he thought. Then he looked for his cell phone to check the time, but it was missing. Joshua looked but could not find it.

Joshua sat up and called out for Susy. There was no

answer. Maybe she had gone downstairs. The hotel served a breakfast. He still could not find his cell phone, but he went to the bathroom to wash up, and pulled on his shirt and pants. Then he realized that his wallet was also missing. He called to Susy again.

Slowly, reality dawned on Joshua. Susy was gone. So was his cell phone and his wallet. Joshua felt foolish as he made his way down to the front desk. He had been scammed. Still hopeful that she was at breakfast downstairs, he asked the lady at the front desk, "Did you see a young woman leave? Pretty, with blond curls."

The desk clerk confirmed his fears. "I saw her. She left several hours ago."

Joshua fought back tears as he said, "She stole my wallet. And she stole my cell phone." Joshua asked the clerk to call the police. Then he thought about his parents. His looked at the clock in the lobby. It was 10:30 in the morning. His dad would be in services and could not be disturbed. He asked the clerk, "Can I use the phone to call my mom?" How would he tell her? There was no choice, he would have to tell the truth and face the consequences.

The police arrived moments later. By the time Marcia arrived, the police had been speaking to him for more than a half hour in the lobby. The detective, a black women who seemed too young to be a detective, was speaking. "Her name is not Susy. Her real name is Lorraine Smith. She is a professional con artist. You are not the first to be scammed by her. And sad to say, you will probably not be the last. We are trying to catch her. I recommend you call your bank immediately and cancel the credit card." The detective wrote up a report and left him to his mom.

His mom gave him a hug and he said he was all right, shook up but not hurt. Marcia had the wisdom to know that his son was hurting, and a hotel lobby was not the place to lecture him. "We need to call the bank. But first I want to reach your father." She stepped away from her son.

Rabbi Williams felt his phone vibrate during religious services. He usually would not answer the phone, but when he saw that his wife was calling, he walked out to return the call. Marcia would only call him in an emergency. She told him the gist of the story, and then said to tell the synagogue there was an urgent family matter. He should leave services immediately and come to the downtown hotel. Then she told him in a harsh voice, "Efraim, enough. It is time to stop teaching that class."

He answered, impatiently, "I think this proves that we need this class more than ever."

When Rabbi Williams arrived at the hotel, they called the bank. It was Saturday morning, so they sat on hold with the bank for almost an hour. When they got through, over $500 had been charged to his card at the mall. Fortunately, the bank was able to cancel the transaction. It would take several weeks to get an appointment and replace his driver's license. Joshua hoped his parents agreed to split the cost of a new phone. But it would take months if not years before he could trust people again.

When they arrived home, Joshua was sure his dad would yell at him. Before his dad could speak, Joshua said, "Dad, I am sorry.

What you said in the class is absolutely true. I guess I did not take it seriously. To have sex, at least according to the Bible, is to know someone. I should not have uncovered myself to another person until I knew her. I made a mistake. I guess it takes time to trust someone. And I trusted a total stranger. I am sorry."

Rabbi Williams was tempted to scold his son further, but what was the point? His son had been through enough. "Joshua, thank God you are ok. I think you learned a lesson. I am sorry you went through this. Remember, whatever happens, you can always call Mom and me."

Joshua hugged his dad as tears filled his eyes.

16. EIGHTH CLASS
THE MARITAL BEDROOM

The first Monday after winter break, all of my students showed up for class except Miriam Pollack. There was a rumor that Miriam's parents had withdrawn her from the school, although I heard nothing officially. Miriam's friend Katy was there, looking nervous. I had an appointment to meet with her after class.

My son Joshua was unusually subdued as he entered the room. He wanted to keep the events of last Friday night secret, but by Monday everybody knew. His friend Isar had a big mouth. Some of the boys congratulated him. "Way to go, Joshua. You are no longer a secondary virgin." Others, both boys and girls, felt bad for him. One girl told him, "I hope you do not believe that all girls are like that." Joshua simply remained silent, hoping the whole incident would go away.

I had to start class. 'Today we are reaching the top of our ladder of holiness, speaking about the marital bedroom. What does Judaism say about sex between a husband and wife?"

Immediately Heather spoke out, "I don't care. I am never getting married. Marriage is a patriarchal institution."

Shmuel responded, "Heather, cut the feminist crap."

Lewis also spoke up, "Heather, let the rabbi speak."

I felt a need to respond. "Why is marriage a patriarchal institution?"

"It treats women like chattel. Imagine a man buying a woman in this day and age. Isn't that what happens at the Jewish wedding ceremony, the man buys the woman."

"We are getting off the subject, but Heather, let me respond. The rabbis do use the Hebrew term *kinyan* for a wedding, a word that usually refers to buying property. But here the man hands the woman something of value, today we use a ring, and the woman accepts it of her own free will. When I buy a piece of property, I do not hand money to the property. But when I was married, I gave Marcia a ring. And to make things even more equal, she also gave me a ring. It is as if we acquired each other as husband and wife. Nobody bought anything.

"According to Talmud, you do not need a ring or anything of value to get married. A man can marry a woman by handing her a document. Today we symbolize that with the *ketubah*. Or a man can marry a woman with the sexual act. Of course, there must be two witnesses."

"In the room?" Gary asked. The class broke out in laughter.

I smiled. "Of course, not in the room. Outside the door. Today we still do this symbolically. As we learned earlier, at a wedding, a couple has a few moments of privacy in a room with witnesses outside the door. It is called *yihud*, from a word meaning *alone*. There was a time when the marriage was literally consummated. Today it is simply their only moment of privacy. But it is a powerful symbol. Among religious Jews, it is forbidden for an unmarried couple to be in a closed room together. This symbolizes their new status, that what was forbidden is now permitted."

Heather would not give up. "I still believe the whole institution is patriarchal."

I looked at her. "Ok, Heather. If it is patriarchal, let me ask you a question? When a couple is married, who has the obligation when it comes to sex and who has the right when it comes to sex."

Heather answered, "Of course, sex is a man's right and a woman's obligation."

"Wrong! By Jewish law, a man has an obligation, and a woman has rights. In the Torah it says it explicitly. A man must provide his wife's food, clothing, and sexual rights."

Heather replied, "Why can't a woman provide her own food and clothing?"

I answered, "She can. But in Torah times, women could not simply get a job. In a marriage a man was obligated to provide. And that includes providing sexual rights. In fact, the Talmud goes into detail, almost too much detail, on how regular these sexual rights are. For a man of leisure, every night."

"My dad is retired, I am going to tell him that," Gary

cracked.

"For a working man, twice a week. For donkey drivers, once a week. For camel drivers, once a month, for sailors, once every six months." Again, the class giggled. "We can laugh, but this is relevant even today. Most of your parents are not ass drivers or camel drivers. But many have jobs where they often travel on business. If a man wishes to take a new job which makes him less available for regular sexual activity, his wife has veto power. It is his duty and her right."

"This law is called *onah* and deals with regular sexual pleasure. There is another rule. A man is obligated to be sure that his wife has pleasure in the sexual act. The rabbis taught that her pleasure comes before his." Now the class was actively listening.

Again, Gary spoke. "How can you talk about pleasure in the sexual act? I heard that Orthodox Jews have sex through a hole in the sheet."

"Gary, we have a word for that – *bubbameisa*, an old wive's tale. It is nonsense, not true. The Talmud says explicitly that sex should be in the nude." Even as I said this, I could not believe I was speaking to a group of students at a Jewish religious school. "Sex is in the nude. Of course, the rabbis do recommend that it be done in the dark, so that one cannot see one's partner's blemishes or be embarrassed by one's own blemishes. None of us have the perfect bodies of supermodels and star athletes. But all of this shows that the rabbis did not shy away from speaking about sexual matters within a marriage."

Now Gary asked a serious question. "Doesn't Judaism require the missionary position? Man on top and woman underneath."

"No. Judaism allows any position, as long as both partners agree. It even allows what the rabbi call *biah sh'lo k'darka*, `sex where semination is not in the usual place.'"

"Rabbi, are you talking about oral sex?"

"What do think semination not in the usual place means?"

Gary spoke out, "My parents told me, when Bill Clinton was president, he said oral sex is not really sex." Again, the class giggled.

"It is really sex. Judaism allows a variety of positions. It forbids sex when one partner is drunk, or one hates the other. It also forbids the husband from forcing himself on his wife against her will."

"Isn't that rape?"

"That is rape. Many legal systems permit marital rape. A husband can force himself on his wife. Jewish law absolutely forbids it." I paused for a minute, letting the class digest these liberal rulings about the marital bedroom.

"I want to speak for a few moments of one other issue." I showed them a picture of steps leading down into an indoor pool. "What is this?"

Someone answered, "A jacuzzi?"

"It looks like a jacuzzi. But it is a mikvah, a Jewish ritual bath. There is an entire area of Jewish law known as *taharat hamishpacha* or family purity. It is strictly practiced by Orthodox Jews, but many non-Orthodox Jews are rediscovering this law. When a woman has her monthly period, she and her husband separate and avoid sex. Then after a period of time, she immerses herself in the mikvah. The Torah say they should separate for seven days. But in the Orthodox world they keep a stricter standard, separating for about twelve days. That puts mikvah night around the time when the woman is most fertile."

Heather remarked, "So you believe women are unclean when they have their period?"

"Heather, I never said that. The Hebrew word is *tamai* meaning ritually impure. When a person is *tamai*, they have to avoid certain holy activities. For example, a person who was *tamai* could not enter the ancient Temple in Jerusalem. When the woman goes to the mikvah, she become *tahor*, ritually pure. She can participate in holy activities – like sex. In Judaism, sex is holy. It is at the top of that ladder of holiness we spoke about in an earlier class. The laws of family purity are complex, and I simply scratched the surface. But couples who observe these laws claim that they make sex within a marriage holy. In fact, in the Talmud, Rabbi Meir taught that on mikvah night a husband sees his wife like a new bride. That is the Jewish view of sex. How do you make sex not only ethical, but holy? How do you climb that ladder of holiness?"

"Rabbi," Lewis asked. "You keep speaking of this ladder of holiness. Where does that come from? My parents were religious Christians who became religious Jews. I discussed this with them.

In all honesty, they disagreed with you. They said sexual activity is black or white, forbidden or permitted. There are no greys, nothing halfway up a ladder."

"Remember when you, Heather, and my son did your academic project presentation at the state capitol? You spoke about memes. A meme is to culture what a gene is to nature. In nature, certain genes develop and flourish while others die out. Similarly in a culture, certain memes develop and flourish while others die out. I want to see the meme of the ladder of holiness flourish. I think our culture, particularly when it comes to sexual behavior, lacks that sense of holiness."

I continued, "I do not know if this meme will take off. It is too easy to say – 'permitted,' 'forbidden.' As you put it, 'black and white.' I did not invent the idea of a ladder of holiness. In fact, it is an old Hasidic idea.

"A Rebbe, a Hasidic leader, once asked his students, two people are on a ladder, one on the second rung and one on the ninth rung. Who is higher? The students all answered, the one on the ninth rung. The Rebbe said, wrong. Who is higher? It is not on which rung you are standing now, but whether you are going up or down the ladder. What matters is which direction you are going.

It does not matter whether one starts higher or lower, as long as they are going up. In fact, then we light Hanukkah candles we increase the number each day from one to eight. The great sage Hillel said one must always go up in holiness and not come down in holiness. That is all for today."

Based on the experience with my son, with Miriam Pollack, and with David Eisenberg, I am not sure that my students were getting the message of my holiness ladder. Now Katy Roberts wanted to see me.

17. THE ABORTION CLINIC

When the other students had left, Katy asked Rabbi Williams, "Can I close the door?"

The rabbi answered, "As I said in class, I don't like being in a closed room alone with someone, particularly a young lady. Let us leave the door ajar. No one can hear us."

He sat down and she pulled up a chair. "Katy, tell me what I can do for you."

She seemed deeply sad, "Rabbi, what does Judaism say about abortion?'

"Are you pregnant, Katy?"

"I just want to know about Judaism and abortion. My boyfriend tells me abortion is murder. Is it?"

The rabbi had not known that Katy had a boyfriend. She always seemed so quiet and shy, particularly next to her friend Miriam.

"Katy, I will answer your question, but then I want to know why you are asking. Jewish tradition does not consider abortion as murder. The fetus is not fully a person. The commentator Rashi says regarding a fetus, *lav nefest hu* `it is not fully a soul.' In fact, the Torah speaks about a man who causes a woman to miscarry. He must pay a fine. In Judaism you never pay a fine for murder. A human being has no price. Abortion is not murder. This is where Judaism disagrees with the pro-life movement. No rabbi would say that a woman who terminates her pregnancy is a murderer."

"So, Judaism permits abortion?" Katy asked.

"I did not say that. Because it is not murder does not mean it is permitted. Judaism also disagrees with the pro-choice advocates who say that a woman can do what she wants with her own body. In Judaism, our bodies belong to God, not to us. We are not permitted to do what we want. That is why Judaism forbids tattoos. In fact, according to the Talmud, if I give someone permission to break my arm and they do it, they are liable. Even if I gave them permission, my arm does not belong to me. We cannot allow someone to damage our bodies. Our bodies belong to God, and we inhabit them to do God's work."

Katy looked puzzled. "So Judaism disagrees with the pro-life position and the pro-choice position. So where does it stand? I am confused."

"Judaism is far more nuanced, staking out a position in the middle that makes sense. For example, the Talmud says for the first forty days the embryo is mere fluid, a collection of chemicals. Abortion would be permissible during this period. Beyond forty days until birth, the fetus is more than mere fluid. It has a certain standing in Jewish law. But it is not yet fully human. If there is a threat to the mother's life, abortion is not only allowed but required, even up to the moment of birth. She has a full life; the fetus does not.

"In other situations, different rabbis may rule differently. If there is a threat to the mother's health or well-being, most rabbis permit abortion. If the fetus is deformed and its birth would cause great pain to the mother, most rabbis permit abortion. Most rabbis permit abortion in cases of rape or incest. One Orthodox rabbi wrote that a woman is not like mother earth, forced to grow a seed planted in her against her will. But in most cases, where there is not a threat to the mother's health or well-being, most rabbis would quote the Torah where it says,

וּבָחַרְתָּ בַּחַיִּים

Therefore choose life. (Deuteronomy 30:19)

"A fetus is not a full life, but it is a potential life. It cannot be destroyed for casual reasons."

"What if the threat to the mother is that her parents will kill her if they find out?" Katy asked.

"Katy, tell me what is going on? Are you pregnant?"

"Is this conversation confidential?"

"I am forbidden from speaking to anyone, even your parents. Katy, talk to me. Did your boyfriend make you pregnant? The one who believes abortion is murder?"

Katy slowly shook her head yes.

"How far along are you?"

"I don't know. A couple of months. More than 40 days."

Rabbi Williams paused. "Katy, you have to tell your parents. You need them during this time. This is not something you can keep a secret."

"You know my parents. They hate each other. The last time they were in the same room together was at my bat mitzvah. At my graduation they will sit at opposite ends of the auditorium. Then they will have two separate parties. If they find out, each will blame the other. But they will kill me."

She looked at him almost pleading for him. "You say that Judaism permits an abortion if the pregnancy is a threat to the mother's well-being. Having a baby is a threat to me. To my plans. To going to college. To my future. I need to terminate this pregnancy. Even if Nicolas does not like it."

"Nicolas is your boyfriend?"

"Yes," she answered. "He is a religious Catholic. He goes to a Catholic High School and his uncle is a priest. He does not understand why I need to do this."

"Katy, will you give me permission to talk to your parents?"

"No!" She shouted. "They cannot know. No one can know. I will tell Nicolas I had a miscarriage. I need to do this, for me."

"Katy, you may not know that in our state there is a twenty-four-hour waiting period for an abortion. When you go to a clinic, they will do some bloodwork and an ultrasound, but then make you wait overnight. I suppose when they passed that law, they were hoping that after seeing the ultrasound, you would reconsider. Also, currently in our state an abortion is only legal up to 15 weeks. You are within that time, but that law could change at any time. Since the Supreme Court overturned Roe v. Wade, the laws are in flux in every state."

"I understand." Then she grew silent for a moment. "I do not even know how I would get to an abortion clinic. I cannot drive myself and you cannot exactly take an Uber for a surgical procedure. Nicolas would never drive me. He does not believe in abortion. I cannot ask my parents to take me."

"Katy, I want you to reconsider. Talk to your parents. They love you. Let them help you."

"No! My parents cannot know."

"Katy, if you insist on going through with this, I will drive you to the clinic." The moment Rabbi Williams said this, he regretted it. He sensed he had crossed a line.

"Thank you, rabbi. Let me think about it." She hugged him and left the room. He pondered the situation for several minutes. The poor girl was in a dilemma. He debated whether he should call her parents. But he promised her confidentiality. If only she would talk with them before making her decision.

Dr. Judith Baker brought Rabbi Williams into her office in her usual gruff, businesslike manner. He thought, *there is no small talk with this woman. Everything is business.*

She immediately started talking. "Next Monday is the last class in January. That is halfway through the school year. It will have to be your last class. We will not continue into the Spring."

"Can I ask why not? I still have material to cover."

"Rabbi, in all honesty, there are people on the school board who wanted me to stop it immediately. I convinced them to give it one more week, give you a chance to finish whatever topic was open. There are people who felt your class was creating too much trouble for the school."

"What kind of trouble?"

"You know that the Pollacks pulled Miriam and Eddie out of our school. They are sending them to the public high school across town."

"No, I did not know that."

"I thought that since Barry Pollack is president of your synagogue, that he would have told you. The Pollacks were active in the school, as well as major donors. They claim that your class was a big part of the reason they were pulling out. Something happened in your class with their daughter."

Rabbi Williams felt his anger rising. "My class had nothing to do with her pulling out. In fact, I met with Barry Pollack last spring, and he encouraged me to teach this class."

"Something happened that got them very angry. Your class was part of it. I do not need controversy at our school. Rabbi Lebovic has also been complaining about your class. He claims what you are teaching is not Judaism. It is secular, liberal values."

"What I am teaching is not Rabbi Lebovic's Orthodox Judaism. It is a Judaism that is resonant with the real lives led by these kids. It is not part of his life."

She countered, "I understand. But I am trying to run a school here. I do not need controversy. And rabbi, you are creating controversy. Can I ask you, what will be the topic of your last class?"

"I am planning to talk about the Jewish view towards homosexuality. I will talk about being gay and Jewish."

"You are aware that David Eisenberg was beaten up in front of a gay night club. His parents also blamed you and pulled him out of your class."

"I am well aware of that. I rushed to the hospital to see David. You cannot blame me if a young man is beaten up by two thugs in front of a gay nightclub."

"I am not blaming you for what happened to David. I am blaming you for creating controversy in our school. I wish you would avoid the subject of gay sex. It is too controversial. How about finding something else for the last class? If Rabbi Lebovic finds out what you are teaching, he will have a fit."

"I did not realize Rabbi Lebovic was setting curriculum for this school. The issue of gays and lesbians is all over the news. This country now permits gay marriage. There are gay rabbis, even within Orthodoxy. I am not going to speak about being transgender in this class; I was saving that topic for after later in the year. But I cannot avoid the topic of homosexuality and Judaism. It will be my topic."

Dr. Baker thought for a moment. "Rabbi, I am a liberal;

some would call me progressive. I am totally in favor of gay rights, even gay marriage. But I have a school to run. I will not fly a rainbow flag in our school. Many of my parents are not as liberal as you or me. You have young people in your class from the Orthodox synagogue. Be careful what you say to these students. And I ask you, do not come out in favor of gay marriage to these students. You still represent our school."

"Dr. Baker, if you attended my class, you would see that I am hardly a liberal on sexual matters. I come down strongly against casual, recreational sex. But I try to teach sexual ethics in keeping with the reality of the lives of our students. And I believe that David Eisenberg is not the only gay student in our school. Maybe if a rabbi spoke to students about being gay in a compassionate manner, more would be willing to come out of the closet."

"I hate to see what would happen to our school if someone else came out as gay as a result of your class."

The rabbi's reaction was swift, but he tried to keep his voice down. "Doctor, this is not about your school, or should I say, our school. My children go here also. This is about peoples' lives. If my class can help one student deal with his or her sexuality, that is a good thing. Thank you. I will let myself out." It took all of Rabbi William's self-control to keep from slamming the door behind him.

Rabbi Williams was still seething when he arrived home. He wanted to speak with his wife, but she was still at work. But his mood totally changed when he found a letter in his mailbox. It was from David Eisenberg's parents.

Dear Rabbi Williams,

We are writing to apologize. We spoke with our son and he wants to go back into your class. He said that you had nothing to do with him getting the fake ID and going to the gay bar. In fact, he said that you would not have approved. He said you would have told him not to go. Something about a gay bar not being in keeping with the holiness of sex.

We are rejoining the synagogue and sending our son back into your class. As Jewish parents, we are still hurting from our son coming out of the closet as gay. We dreamed that one day he would find a bride, be married under a huppah, and give us grandchildren. But we love our son. And to use his own words, he needs to be the way God created him.

We understand that in the next class, you will be discussing homosexuality and Judaism. If our son allows it, we would like to attend that class. We need to hear some sensible words from a rabbi about how to understand our son. Again, our sincere apology.

Shalom,

Ronald & Julia Eisenberg

Rabbi Williams immediately picked up the phone and called them. He had mixed feelings about parents attending his class. Perhaps the young people would not be so open. But he sensed this was important to them. If David would permit it, he would permit it.

Katy and Miriam sat in Miriam's car across town, waiting for the Women's Health Center to open. Demonstrators were already gathering outside the clinic, holding signs like "Stop Killing Babies" and "Your Baby Has a Heartbeat." Katy tried to ignore the signs, but they troubled her. Rabbi Williams had said that abortion was permitted if pregnancy would cause pain and suffering to the mother. He had even offered to drive her. Katy worried how she would pay for the abortion. She had $400 in her purse of her own money. She knew the procedure would cost more. Miriam had promised to loan her the money if necessary.

She also dreaded the idea of going in for blood work and a sonagram, then coming back tomorrow. She wanted to get it over with. But Miriam had promised to be with her. It was difficult for Katy now that Miriam had transferred to the public school. She appreciated her friend being there for her.

Miriam said, "They are open. We need to go in." Neither girl had told their parents where they were going. They both lied that their schools had a field trip. They knew that no one would recognize them at the clinic. But both girls were extremely uncomfortable.

Katy said, "Can you give me a minute alone? I need to gather my thoughts."

Miriam respected her friend and stood outside, leaving Katy alone in the car. After a few moments, she saw Katy pick up her cell phone.

Katy texted Nicolas, saying that she needed to speak to him immediately. A minute later, the phone rang. It was Nicolas' voice. "I am in school. I had to sneak out to the restroom. What is happening, Katy?"

"When you said that you would marry me this summer and raise our child together, did you really mean it?"

"Katy, I love you. I mean it with all my heart. I want to marry you."

"Nicolas, over the weekend, if I can arrange it, would you be willing to meet my parents?"

"Tell me when and I will be there."

"I love you, Nicolas." And she hung up. She signaled Miriam to come back to the car. "Miriam, thank you. I am not going through with this. Can you drive me back to school? I need to make two phone calls." With her hand shaking, she called her mom and then her dad. "I need to speak with the two of you together. It is important." Both her parents agreed to meet at her mom's home at 2 pm Saturday afternoon. She texted Nicolas back. "Be at my home 2 pm Saturday." Then she breathed a sigh of relief. She had made a decision.

It was already 2:15 Saturday afternoon at Katy's mom's home, and they were still waiting for her dad. Nicolas had come at 2 and Katy had introduced him to her. "Nicholas, this is my Mom, Fran Roberts. Mom, this is my boyfriend, Nicholas Velazzi."

Nicholas courteously shook her hand, but Fran looked surprised. She did not know her daughter had a boyfriend. Katy said nothing about why she wanted to meet. Her mom said, "Your Dad is always late. Why did you invite him anyway?"

"Mom, he is my dad. We will wait for him." Katy was stoic, but Nicolas was fidgety, quite nervous. He knew that later in the day they would have the same meeting with his parents. His parents would be upset, but he knew his family ties were stronger than Katy's. They could get through it. He was worried about Katy, and about the difficult relationship she had with her parents.

Finally, Katy's dad showed up, without an apology for being late. He kissed his daughter and ignored his ex-wife. He looked at Nicolas, and Katy said, "Nicholas, this is my dad, Warren Roberts. Dad, this is my boyfriend, Nicholas Velazzi."

Again, Nicholas courteously shook his hand. Warren seemed less surprised that Katy had a boyfriend. She lived with her mom most of the time, so her dad was less familiar with the details of her life.

Katy said, "Let's sit down. We need to talk." She had been frightened about this meeting but now felt a deep inner strength. Katy's mom brought out a pitcher of iced tea and the four of them sat around the kitchen table. Nicholas was surprised how calm Katy appeared as she began to speak.

"Mom, Dad, Nicolas has been my boyfriend for the last four months. We have been meeting secretly, texting, speaking on the phone, going out and having long talks, mostly about religion.

Nicolas is a senior at St. Anselm High School. He comes from a strong Catholic family; his uncle is a priest. For the first time in my life, I have found someone whom I love. And Nicolas loves me. We are totally comfortable with each other."

Fran spoke, obviously upset, "We sent you to that Jewish school, which costs us a fortune, so you would meet Jewish boys. There are no boys at your school you can date?" She looked at Nicholas. "Nicholas, no insult intended. You seem like a nice young man. But Katy knows how we feel about interfaith dating."

"Mom and Dad, we are not just dating. We are engaged. We plan to be married after we graduate in the spring."

Warren stood up, aghast, "No way! You are not getting married. You are both far too young."

Katy kept her voice calm although her stomach was churning. "We are not too young. We will both be eighteen by the summer and can legally be married. We do not need your permission, although it would be nice if you give us your blessing."

Warren was stunned by her words. "Our blessing! You will only be eighteen. You have a whole life ahead of you. College, a career. How will you two support yourselves with only a high school education?"

"Dad, this is not about college. We are both planning to go to college. This is about love. We are going to get married."

Warren continued, "What about religion? He is a religious Catholic." Warren spoke as if Nicholas were not sitting there. "You are a Jew. What kind of home will you have? A *menorah* in the window and a Christmas tree in the living room? A wreath and a *mezuzah* on the door? A baptism and a *bris* for your kids?" He was now shouting.

Katy remained calm. "Dad, there is no need to shout. We love each other and can work out all those issues." Nicholas was amazed at how Katy was handling this.

Now Warren turned to his ex-wife. "Fran, did you know about this relationship?"

Fran replied, "I am as a surprised as you are. Maybe if you were a bit more involved in Jewish life, this would not have happened. I was the one that brought her to synagogue, had the holiday dinners, insisted on the Jewish school."

Warren seemed to jump out of his skin. "Who paid for that Jewish school? You had her most weekends, most holidays. Of course, you were more involved in Judaism than me." Katy knew that her parents would start fighting, and knew she had to stop it.

"Mom, Dad, stop! I love being Jewish. Nicholas loves being Catholic. And we love each other. We are getting married."

Warren took a moment and calmed down, "Who will do this wedding? You know Rabbi Williams is forbidden to do interfaith weddings. He will not perform a wedding between a Jew and a Catholic."

Nicolas finally felt comfortable speaking, "As Katy said, my uncle is a priest. He has done interfaith weddings. We will also have a rabbi there; Katy would want that. Our religions are important to both of us. I understand your rabbi cannot do it. But I am sure there are rabbis out there who will join with a priest and sanctify our marriage. I love your daughter. I want to make her happy. I will take care of her."

Now Fran spoke. "Why the rush? Why this summer? Wait a couple years. You have only known each other a few months. Why not give it time? Finish two years of college. Get to know each other better."

Katy paused, then spoke softly. "Mom, Dad. There is something else we have to tell you. I'm pregnant." She paused to let the news sink in. "We are going to have a baby. Both Nicolas and I want the baby to be born to a married couple. That is why we plan to be married right after graduation."

Both Fran and Warren sat in stunned silence. Then Warren confronted Fran again. "Did you know our daughter was sexually active? Didn't you think to put her on the pill?"

Fran reacted strongly. "I did not know she was sexually active. I didn't even know she was dating! And I would not have approved of her having sex. Do not blame me. You are well aware that we both agreed to sign her up for the sexual ethics class taught by Rabbi Williams. Obviously that did not do any good."

Again, Katy had to intervene, "Mom, Dad, stop it. I love Rabbi Williams' class. But Nicholas and I chose to have sex. We are seventeen, not children."

Nicholas watched this fighting back and forth, speechless. His family would never have such conflicts.

Fran spoke to her daughter. "You are too young to have a

baby. And you are too young to be married. We are going to arrange an abortion."

Nicolas immediately reacted, "Abortion is murder."

Katy put her hand on his arm to stop him from speaking further. "Mom and Dad, I almost had an abortion. Miriam drove me to the clinic. I spoke with Rabbi Williams about it. The rabbi said that Jewish law permits abortion if the pregnancy will cause pain and suffering to the mother. Rabbi Williams even offered to drive me to the abortion clinic." Katy regretted her words the minute she said them. She realized that she had just thrown her Rabbi under the bus.

Katy's dad reacted with fury, "Our Rabbi offered to drive our daughter to an abortion clinic. Without consulting us." Rabbi Williams was not his Rabbi. Since the divorce, only his mother belonged to the synagogue.

"I would not allow Rabbi Williams to tell you. I only shared my pregnancy with him on the grounds that our meeting would be totally confidential. In truth, he tried to convince me to speak to you. He tried several times. He even offered to call you himself. When I refused, he offered to help me. But when I arrived at the clinic, I changed my mind. Abortion is permitted if it causes pain and suffering to the mother. This pregnancy does not cause pain and suffering to me, but rather brings me joy. I think of the family that Nicolas and I are going to create."

Fran spoke again, "What about having the baby and placing it for adoption?"

"Mom, I have friends who are adopted. They have wonderful parents who raised them. But they always wonder who gave birth to them and why those birth parents gave them up. I am not having an abortion and I am not placing our baby for adoption. Nicolas and I are getting married this summer. We will raise our baby together. We want you there, but we will be married whether you are there or not. But at a time like this, I need you. Both of you." With that, Katy had said everything she needed to say. She felt her energy drain out of her.

Fran and Warren were silent. They did not know what to say. Then they looked at one another. First Fran and then Warren stood up and hugged her. They each shook hands with Nicolas. Then something unbelievable happened. Fran and Warren gave each other a hug. Katy's news had broken the barrier between them. The visit continued for a brief while, until Katy said, "We need to leave. We have to speak to Nicolas' parents."

18. NINTH CLASS
GAY AND JEWISH

I was pleasantly surprised to see perfect attendance for my last class. I guess they knew the controversy regarding my subject. Every student was there except, of course, Miriam Pollack, who had transferred Taft High School. I still felt bad over how things had turned out with her. But I did not feel guilty. I believe that by respecting her confidentiality, I had acted according to my professional ethics. But that did not protect me from Barry and Susan Pollack's anger. I doubt they would ever forgive me.

David Eisenberg was sitting next to his parents Ronald and Julia. I do not know who looked more nervous: David, having his parents present, or his parents, sitting in a classroom with a group of teenagers. I was ready to begin when the door opened, and in walked Dr. Judith Baker. She took a seat and said, "Rabbi, I hope you do not mind if I join you. I would like to see the class."

I did mind; I was never comfortable in her presence. But it was time to go ahead.

"Today we are going to talk about being gay and Jewish.

We are going to be quite specific, describing certain sexual acts. I hope you are comfortable with that." One of the girls giggled but I ignored it. "Let me start with a question. Can someone be a strictly observant Jew, following all of Jewish laws, and be gay?"

Shmuel immediately answered. "Of course not. The Torah forbids it. Rabbi Lebovic says that book of Leviticus forbids people from being gay."

"I must respectfully disagree. I am afraid Rabbi Lebovic is wrong about this. Being gay is about desire or attraction. Someone who is sexually attracted to members of their own sex. A man is sexually attracted to men, or a woman is sexually attracted to women. Judaism is not about desire; it is about action. If a person does not act on their sexual attraction, they have not broken any Jewish law. A man can be sexually attracted only to other men, never act on it, and be a one-hundred-percent Orthodox observant Jew.

"This is an issue on which Judaism differs from Christianity. In Christianity, thoughts matter. The New Testament teaches, *But I tell you that anyone who looks at a woman lustfully has already committed adultery in his heart* (Matthew 5:28). It was before your time, but in 1976 when Jimmy Carter was running for president, he was interviewed by *Playboy* Magazine. Carter commented that through the years he had committed adultery in his heart. There was a huge backlash among Christian voters. But most Jews shrugged it off. Adultery is about what someone does with their body, not what someone feels in their heart. Judaism forbids certain actions, not certain thoughts."

"Are you saying gays need to be celibate to be good Jews?" Gary Brown challenged me.

"I am not saying that at all. Judaism forbids certain activities. We need to look at what those activities are and why Judaism forbids them. Judaism does not forbid inner feelings or desires."

I continued, "Let us look at two verses in Leviticus, which seems to give everybody so much trouble." I passed out a paper with the two verses and a comment from the medieval commentator Rashi:

וְאֶת־זָכָר לֹא תִשְׁכַּב מִשְׁכְּבֵי אִשָּׁה תּוֹעֵבָה הִוא:

"Do not lie with a male as one lies with a woman; it is an abhorrence" (Leviticus 18:22).

וְאִישׁ אֲשֶׁר יִשְׁכַּב אֶת־זָכָר מִשְׁכְּבֵי אִשָּׁה תּוֹעֵבָה עָשׂוּ שְׁנֵיהֶם מוֹת יוּמָתוּ דְּמֵיהֶם בָּם:

"If a man lies with a male as one lies with a woman, the two of them have done an abhorrent thing; they shall be put to death—their bloodguilt is upon them" (Leviticus 20:13).

מִשְׁכְּבֵי אשה מַכְנִיס כְּמִכְחוֹל בִּשְׁפוֹפֶרֶת.

"'As one lies with a woman.' As if he inserts a makeup brush into a tube" (Rashi on Leviticus 20:13).

"There are two verses, both of which forbid one kind of behavior. We read the first of these verses on Yom Kippur afternoon. In fact, some liberal synagogues have changed the Yom

190

Kippur reading so they do not need to read this verse. In my synagogue we read the traditional reading. These verses are in the middle of a long section dealing with forbidden sexual relations, particularly incest and bestiality. But the section also forbids sex with a woman during her menstrual period, as well as child sacrifices. People focus on two verses about men having sex with men and ignore all the other issues raised by the book of Leviticus. Let us look carefully at the two verses. What do they say?"

We studied both verses together in the Hebrew and English. "Some people translate the word *toevah* not as *abhorrent* but *abomination*. I do not like either word. I find them too harsh. I prefer the word *mistake*, which is the way the Talmud translates it. The Talmud says *toeh ata ba, you go astray on account of it.*

I continued, "So what is the Torah saying is forbidden?"

"Homosexuality," someone answered.

"Look more closely. It prohibits something very specific." I was silent for a moment. "Both verses say that a man should not lie with a man *as he lies with a woman.* What does that mean? Rashi, who was the greatest medieval rabbinic commentator, gives the answer in his commentary, *as if he inserts a makeup brush into a tube.* What does that mean?"

I imagine that the class was surprised that I would explicitly describe such a sexual encounter. "Rashi is talking about penetration. When a man has sex with a woman, this includes penetration. The Torah is saying that a man should not penetrate another man the way he might penetrate a woman. But why?

"Think about the time when the Torah was written. Women had a secondary role. Men had the power. For a man to penetrate another man was to treat him as a woman, to act as he had power over him. The Torah forbade men from acting that way. But the world has changed. Judaism has changed. Women are no longer second-class citizens." I was surprised that Heather was silent when I made that statement. "Today we no longer see that fact that a man penetrates a woman as giving her second-class status. In fact, today many women are the ones who initiate sex. With that in mind, perhaps there is room to overturn this prohibition, particularly if there is a good reason."

Now Lewis spoke up, "I thought homosexuality is forbidden in Judaism because of what happened in Sodom. Lot hid the two visitors to Sodom from a group of men who wanted to rape them. He even offered his daughters in their place. My parents told me, when they heard about the topic, that this is the reason homosexuality is called sodomy. Because of Sodom."

I responded, "That was a case of homosexual rape, not consensual sex. It hardly applies to our topic. Regarding Lot's daughters, it is a very troubling story. It can only say that it shows the importance in those days of hospitality, how far Lot was willing to go to protect visitors to his home. Today among Bedouins and other mid-Eastern nomads there is still that emphasis on hospitality to strangers. Remember it was Lot's daughters who later committed incest with their father to populate the world. But let us return to our story."

Heather spoke up, "Again you are speaking about men and what they are allowed to do or not do. This whole class seems to be about men and what they can do or not do. What about women? Does the Torah speak about lesbians?"

"Heather, since men are obligated to marry and have children while women are not obligated, the Torah focuses on men. But there is one passage in the Talmud about lesbians. If two women give each other pleasure, the Talmud asks whether one of them later marry a *kohen* or priest. A priest could not marry a woman who was sexually promiscuous. Rav Huna says that a priest cannot marry this woman. But Rava says they may marry, such behavior is not considered sexually promiscuous."

Heather gasped, "Why would a lesbian want to marry a priest? Let them marry each other." The class laughed.

"Heather, the Rabbis are simply saying that lesbianism is not promiscuity. They could not even imagine two women marrying each other. But Heather is correct. Much of Rabbinic literature seems to be men talking about men. Women often fade into the background." I had to respect Heather for her passion, even if she was constantly challenging me.

"Let me return to the matter at hand. Suppose a young man comes to me and says, *Rabbi I'm gay. I can only find sexual satisfaction with another man. Yet I want to live a traditional Jewish life. If I decide to marry a woman, it would be unfair to me, and certainly unfair to her.* What should I tell him?

"There are rabbis, even in this day and age, who teach that

he should get psychological counseling to try to change his sexual orientation. There is even a Jewish organization whose goal is to help gays become straight. I am deeply skeptical of such efforts. I believe being gay is a deep part of the human psyche. Whether caused by genetics or upbringing or both, I do not believe it is changeable."

David breathed a sigh of relief as I said that.

"There are rabbis who would say that such a person should live a life of celibacy. They are fated by their nature to live a life alone, without a sexual partner. But I do not agree. The Torah says, *It is not good for man to be alone.* People need a partner. To be fated to live one's life without ever seeking love strikes me as deeply sad.

"That is the reason I would tell gay men or lesbians to seek out a sexual partner. The same rules apply as for a straight couple. Get to know the person before opening up to them. Be honest with them. Practice fidelity. Know them in a Biblical sense. In this way, I believe gay people as well as straight people can climb the holiness ladder."

David nervously raised his hand. "First, everybody, I want to thank my parents for coming. They know I am gay. You also know I am gay. Rabbi. I appreciate your support if I look for a serious partner. No more gay bars for me." Again the class laughed. "Rabbi, let me suppose I find a such a partner, we are in love, and in a faithful relationship. Let me suppose he is Jewish."

David's mom said, "From your mouth to God's ears." I had

to smile.

David continued, "And suppose, since it is legal for gays to marry, we apply for a marriage license. Then we come to you. You are my rabbi. Would you perform my wedding?"

I should have expected the question. Whatever I answered, there would be trouble. I had been thinking about this question for years. Now it was time to answer. But I had to answer honestly. "David, when you meet the right man and fall in love, if he is Jewish and you get a proper marriage license, I would perform your wedding." I had said it.

Then something surprising happened. The class applauded. At least, everyone but Shmuel.

Dr. Butler immediately stood up. "Rabbi, I believe the class must end here. Students you can go. The rabbi's sex class is over." She walked out of the room and the students followed.

I should have been angry. Or scared. Or sad. But I felt none of these. I felt an elation. I finally publicly admitted what I had decided privately long ago.

19. THE SYNAGOGUE BOARD

There were eighteen members of the synagogue board, a lucky number that means *chai* "life." As Rabbi Williams sat in the board room, he did not feel any *joy of life*. The number of board members did not include the synagogue president, who for nearly two years had been Barry Pollack. Every board member had shown up, something that never happened, for the 7:30 emergency meeting. They sat around four long tables set up in a square, with a small podium for the president. The board members knew how important this meeting was. Rabbi Williams also knew that his career was on the line. His future with this synagogue would be decided by this group of men and women.

Barry took out a dossier with several papers, like a lawyer would bring into a courtroom. He began, "Thank you for coming to this emergency board meeting. There is only one piece of business on the agenda, whether Rabbi Williams will continue as our spiritual leader." He pulled a piece of paper out of the dossier. "I am going to read a short clause from the rabbi's contract: *The rabbi may be terminated at any time for cause. Cause means being convicted of a felony or misdemeanor. Cause also means any unethical behavior which affects negatively on our synagogue.* I am going to show that, on four occasions over the last few months, the rabbi displayed such improper ethical behavior."

"Four occasions?"

"Rabbi, you will have a chance to respond."

"Mr. Pollack." The rabbi always called him Barry, but now he was Mr. Pollack. "You are an attorney, accustomed to cross examining people in court. My job is on the line. I believe I deserve the right to legal counsel."

"Rabbi, we are not in court; I am not acting as an attorney, but as president of the synagogue. As I said, you will have a chance to respond."

Fred Epstein spoke up. He was the oldest member of the board and had been president when Rabbi Williams assumed the pulpit. "Barry, the Rabbi is right. I think he deserves legal counsel. This entire meeting strikes me as a one-man attack on our Rabbi." Fred had always been a supporter of Rabbi Williams, and he appreciated his words. But it was Barry who was in charge.

Barry responded, "Fred, we will be fair and give Rabbi Williams a chance to respond. As I said, I am going to raise four occasions where the rabbi behaved in a questionable manner."

Barry continued, "Let me begin with the first instance. Did you give your son permission to go to a rock concert on a Friday night?"

Rabbi Williams glared at Barry. "Leave me family out of this. They have nothing to do with this."

Barry ignored him, "Let me tell the board what happened. Your son went to a concert on a Friday night."

"My son is seventeen years old. He will do what he wants."

"He went to a concert. There he picked up a girl and they got a hotel room together. When he woke up the next morning, the girl was gone after robbing him blind. I know the story because I have a copy of the police report here."

The rabbi was amazed that Barry had tracked down the police report. It was the personal business of his family, not the business of the synagogue. He felt like he had to reply, "The woman is a professional thief. She stole his wallet and cell phone. My son felt bad. It is over. It was a painful incident, but it has nothing to do with my performance as a rabbi."

"Rabbi, I believe that when you encourage sexual activity at too young an age, that is what happens. Let me turn to the second incident."

"David Eisenberg, who grew up in this synagogue, bought a fake ID and went to a gay bar. Outside he was jumped by two thugs, who put him in the hospital."

"I hope you are not blaming me for what happened to David. I ran to the hospital the minute I heard."

"I am not blaming you for him going to a gay bar. I am blaming you for the casual acceptance of homosexual behavior when the Torah clearly forbids it. Let me ask you a question, rabbi.

Did you tell your class at Eastman that you were prepared to perform a marriage between two men?"

"Yes, I did say that to the class."

"And don't you think this kind of decision must be made in consultation with the synagogue's religious committee?"

"I do not need the permission of our religious committee to do a wedding."

"When you do a wedding, you represent our synagogue. Gay marriage is controversial in our community. You had an obligation to discuss this with the religious committee before making such a statement. I do not believe that such a vital decision, that could affect the future of the synagogue, should be discussed in front of a group of teens."

Wendy Stern, another board member spoke up. "Our son Steven is in that class; he goes by Shmuel now. He admitted that he disagreed with Rabbi William's statement about gay marriage. But he admitted that, when Rabbi Williams said it, the class applauded. David Eisenberg's parents were there, and even they applauded. Our son loves the class, even when he disagrees with Rabbi Williams. Instead of attacking the Rabbi, you should be praising his courage."

Barry replied, "David Eisenberg's parents at first quit this synagogue and then rejoined. But they were deeply disturbed by the Rabbi's actions. And I still claim that our rabbi should not publicly proclaim that he will perform a gay marriage without first discussing it with our religious committee."

Wendy strongly said, "I support our Rabbi."

Allen Fischer spoke out, "The Rabbi overstepped his bounds. Let Barry continue." Allen was one of the younger members of the board, with three children in the synagogue's religious school. He was an accountant, who served as treasurer of the synagogue.

Barry barreled on. "Let me raise a third situation. This involved my own daughter Miriam."

The Rabbi stood up. "I told you that I cannot discuss any confidential conversations I had with anyone. Even if I had a conversation with your daughter, and I am not saying I did, I will not discuss it. This issue has no place at this meeting."

Barry took another piece of paper out of the dossier. "I am holding a note, signed by my daughter, giving me permission to discuss her conversation with the rabbi. The note is notarized by my law partner. So the entire incident is no longer confidential."

The rabbi drew a breath but did not speak.

"Sadly, my daughter posed for a picture with a revealing pose and sent it to her former boyfriend. She shared this information with the rabbi, who chose not to tell us and not to call the boyfriend, a young man from this synagogue. When my daughter broke up with her boyfriend, he posted the picture on social media. My daughter is still embarrassed. We were forced to pull her and her brother out of the Eastman Jewish Academy and send her to another school across town. The Rabbi could have stopped this with a call to us. But he refused."

Rabbi Williams spoke, "I was sworn to confidentiality by your daughter. I would have broken my own code of professional ethics if I had spoken to anyone about our conversation. Congregants need to know that they can share secrets with me and I will respect their privacy."

Barry took out another piece of paper. "Now for the most egregious of all. I have a second notarized note permitting me to reveal a conversation the Rabbi had with another young person from our synagogue, Katy Roberts. Katy's mother is a member of our congregation." The other situations were familiar to the board, but they knew nothing about Katy. Barry turned to the rabbi. "Did Katy share with you that she was pregnant, and that she was considering having an abortion?"

Rabbi Williams knew that it was useless keeping silent. Katy had signed a paper. "She asked me what Judaism teaches about abortion."

"And did you tell her that such an abortion is permissible?"

"I told her to discuss it with her parents."

"When Katy said that she would not discuss it with her parents, did you offer to drive her to the abortion clinic?"

Rabbi Williams looked at the faces of the board members when Barry made that statement, and he sensed it was over.

Barry continued, "You offered to drive a young woman, still a minor, to an abortion clinic in order to avoid telling her parents?" The rabbi let out a long slow breath but chose not to answer. "I believe that these incidents show a pattern of ethical behavior by our rabbi which is detrimental to the synagogue. It is my opinion that this board ought to consider immediate termination. But I am ready to let Rabbi Williams respond."

Before the rabbi could say anything, Ellie Reynolds, one of the few people of color in the synagogue, spoke up. "I need to say something in the rabbi's defense. I rarely speak out at these meetings. My son Lewis is in the rabbi's class. As you know, my whole family was Baptist. We all converted with Rabbi Williams. We are certainly one of the more observant families in the synagogue, coming to services every Friday night and every Saturday morning. And our son Lewis takes his Judaism seriously. He loves the rabbi's class. Lewis says that while many of his classmates are sexually active, he has chosen to wait. Rabbi Williams gave him the arguments he needs to maintain such a traditional stance. I am proud of our rabbi, and our family thinks his class served an important purpose."

Then Rabbi Williams spoke, "Thank you, Ellie. I am not going to answer these four charges, because I think they are unfair. Confidential conversations I had with teenagers are not the business of this board. You ought to be proud that our teens are willing to talk to me. I only want to answer one charge – that I encourage sexual promiscuity among high school students. I totally deny that charge. In fact, I am doing the opposite. I have told these young people over and over to wait. I have told them not to uncover themselves for someone else until they are in a mature, loving, faithful relationship. I have taught them that sex is holy and that casual, recreational sex is wrong. I have told them to climb a ladder of holiness regarding sexual behavior. Obviously, it is a message they needed to hear. And they needed to hear it from a rabbi. I hope you will let me continue my work here, but I will respect the decision of this board."

Barry refused to look at the rabbi. "We will now go into executive session and make a decision. Rabbi, you can leave. I will call you after the board meeting."

The phone rang in the Williams home less than an hour later. "Rabbi, the board voted to terminate your contract effective immediately. The vote was 13 to 5. I am sorry it came to this. We have worked well together but I believe you used poor judgement. I believe the board had no choice."

Rabbi Williams was not surprised. He turned to his wife and said, "It is over."

Barry continued. "They did agree that if you write a letter of resignation, they will pay you severance. Since you are being terminated for cause, they are not obligated to pay it. I believe this is gracious of them."

"Barry, I will drop a letter of resignation off at your office tomorrow. I do need a few days to pack up my books and clean out my office."

"No problem."

It had been a good job, a busy synagogue for an energetic rabbi. And now it was over. Rabbi Williams smiled at Marcia.

"Time to start planning the next stage of our lives."

Marcia did not return the smile; the look of anger in her eyes said it all. "I was against you teaching that class from the beginning." She turned and walked away from him.

EPILOGUE

Three months had gone by since I dropped off my letter of resignation to Barry Pollack. It had taken a week to pack up my books and other belongings in my office. I had returned my keys and they had changed all the computer passwords so that I no longer had access to anything synagogue related. I had not set foot in the building since then; in fact, I began going to services Shabbat morning at Rabbi Lebovic's Orthodox synagogue. Many of the members of my former synagogue called me, dropped me emails, or sent letters expressing their regrets. But it was over. Fortunately, between the severance and Marcia's job, we had earned enough money to survive.

I had received a job offer at another synagogue, in another state, over a thousand miles away, less money and less prestige, but a job none the less. Now I was finishing the packing for the move. Marcia and our daughter Shira were already in the new community, looking for a home to rent. Marcia told me that she needed some time away from me, to contemplate the future of our marriage. Shira complained bitterly about the move, and about the fact that she would be transferring to a public high school. But when she learned that her new high school had both a lacrosse and track team, she became excited. She was sure she could make the team. We told her there was no choice. Besides, she was outgoing and would make new friends.

Joshua would stay behind, going to college in our state. He would live with Isar for the next month, then Marcia and I would fly back for his graduation and to move him into his new dorm for the summer term. Meanwhile, I was calling people from the new synagogue, learning names and making acquaintances.

Now the moving van had come to take our furniture. Joshua and I were loading up my car with some last boxes of books, papers, and other belongings. I was amazed how much material one could acquire living in a community for over fifteen years. As we were carrying boxes, a car came down the road and stopped in front of our house. Out stepped a very pregnant Katy Roberts.

I knew that Katy always thought of herself as the ugly duckling next to her pretty friend Miriam. She used to say she was the Leah next to Miriam's Rachel, a Biblical reference to the homely older sister with the weak eyes. But today her eyes had a glow. With her large belly and her big smile, she looked positively radiant.

Katy and Nicolas would be married in a few weeks, anxious to have the wedding before the baby was born. Her mom and dad had set aside their mutual hatred, working together to help her plan the wedding. Nicolas' uncle, the priest, would perform the wedding, together with a local free-lance rabbi who was not part of any national rabbinic association. I had little respect for such rabbis, who earned their living performing interfaith marriages. But as I looked at Katy, I am glad that our traditions would be represented at the wedding.

About two months after the wedding, she would give birth to a baby boy. She would give him a bris, circumcising the baby and bringing him into the covenant of Abraham. Nicolas had agreed to that. Shortly afterwards he would be brought to Nicolas' church and baptized, brought into the faith of Jesus. Katy had agreed to that. The baby would be raised as a Jew and as a Christian. I had no idea how that would work. They did not ask my opinion and I did not say anything. They would have to figure it out as they went along. But I knew that Katy was in love.

She walked over to me. "Rabbi, I have something for you." It was a card, and when I opened it, a gift certificate from an online bookstore fell out: $360 to spend on books. My library would keep growing.

"Read the card, rabbi." It was a thank you card one could buy in a supermarket. But inside was a note:

"Dear Rabbi Williams,

Please accept this gift from all of us in appreciation of the wonderful class you taught on sexual ethics. You inspired each of us to become better human beings and better Jews."

It was followed by a list of signatures.

"Nicolas helped me pick out the card and write the message. I gathered the signatures," Katy said.

I looked at the names of those who signed the card. First was my own son Joshua Williams. Then his best friend Isar Amir, whose parents originally forbade him from taking the class. The signatures continued. There was Heather Hall, whose strident feminism challenged me in almost every class. I hope she would find a way to channel that passion into improving the world. And then there was Shmuel, who challenged me from the opposite side, displaying his Orthodoxy.

There was David Eisenberg, whose parents had pulled him from the class after the incident in the gay bar, and then joined him for the final class. He had come a long way in the last few months. David had met with the board of the school and received permission to form the Pride Club, a club at the school for LGBTQ students and their supporters. Rabbi Lebovic fought the new club bitterly. He said it was against Jewish law and tradition. When it was formed anyway, he resigned his position as the Judaica teacher. He could not teach in a school that undermined the laws of the Torah. In a way, I felt sorry for him. He believed what he believed. But the school needed a Judaica teacher more in touch with the reality of these students' lives.

There was a signature from Gary Brown, who loved to argue with me on almost every point. And there was a signature of Lewis Reynolds. I still appreciate the way his mother stood up for me at that board meeting. There were several other signatures. And then

I saw one from Katy Roberts, followed by something in parentheses. (Soon to be Katy Velazzi.)

I looked, and there was one last signature at the bottom. It included a little note: *Thank you rabbi, Miriam Pollack.* Even Miriam had signed it. Every student in my class had signed. For a moment, my eyes teared up. Perhaps the class in sexual ethics was worth it after all.

When Katy left, Joshua and I brought a few more boxes to the car. I hugged my son goodbye, took one last look at the house, and prepared to get into the car to drive away. My new life was waiting. Then Joshua came walking out carrying one last box. "You forgot this one. I think there is still room in the car."

I looked in the box. It was all the books I had used to prepare for my class. On top was an English translation of Nachmanides *Epistle of Holiness*, a medieval mystical treatise on how a man should treat his wife in the marital bed. Underneath were numerous other books on sexual ethics, including books written by various rabbis. There was *A Hedge of Roses* written by Rabbi Norman Lamm, an Orthodox rabbi, *Does God Belong in the Bedroom?* written by Rabbi Michael Gold, a Conservative rabbi, and *Choosing a Sex Ethic* written by Rabbi Eugene Borowitz, a Reform rabbi. There were several books written by Christian theologians such as *Between Two Gardens* by James B. Nelson. There were even works by secular scholars such as philosopher Thomas Nagel's essay "Sexual Perversion."

Do I need these books? Would I ever teach such a class

again? Or should I tell my son to donate them to the local library? I wavered for a moment. Then I told my son, "Put them in the car. Perhaps I will use them again."

Sources

Prologue

(Talmud *Berakhot* 62a)

Rav Kahana entered and lay beneath Rav's bed. He heard Rav chatting and laughing and seeing to his needs, Rav Kahana said to Rav: The mouth of Abba, Rav, is like one whom has never eaten a cooked dish, Rav said to him: Kahana, you are here? Leave, as this is an undesirable mode of behavior. Rav Kahana said to him: It is Torah, and I must learn.

רַב כָּהֲנָא עָל, גְּנָא תּוּתֵיה פּוּרְיֵיה דְּרַב. שַׁמְעֵיה דְּשָׂח וְשָׂחַק וְעָשָׂה צְרָכָיו. אָמַר לֵיה : דָּמֵי פּוּמֵיה דְּאַבָּא כִּדְלָא שָׂרֵיף תַּבְשִׁילָא. אָמַר לֵיה : כָּהֲנָא, הָכָא אַתְּ? פּוּק, דְּלָאו אֹרַח אַרְעָא. אָמַר לֵיה : תּוֹרָה הִיא, וְלִלְמוֹד אֲנִי צָרִיךְ.

Chapter 1 The Friday Night Party

(Genesis 29:16-17)

Laban had two daughters, the name of the older was Leah and the name of the younger was Rachel. Leah had soft eyes, but Rachel was shapely and beautiful.

וּלְלָבָן שְׁתֵּי בָנוֹת שֵׁם
הַגְּדֹלָה לֵאָה וְשֵׁם
הַקְּטַנָּה רָחֵל : וְעֵינֵי
לֵאָה רַכּוֹת וְרָחֵל הָיְתָה
יְפַת־תֹּאַר וִיפַת מַרְאֶה :

Chapter 2 First Class The Rabbi and the Prostitute

(Numbers 15:38)

Speak to the children of Israel and say to them, make fringes on the corners of their garments for all generations, and put on the fringes a thread of blue.

דַּבֵּר אֶל־בְּנֵי יִשְׂרָאֵל
וְאָמַרְתָּ אֲלֵהֶם וְעָשׂוּ
לָהֶם צִיצִת עַל־כַּנְפֵי
בִגְדֵיהֶם לְדֹרֹתָם וְנָתְנוּ
עַל־צִיצִת הַכָּנָף פְּתִיל
תְּכֵלֶת :

(Talmud *Menachot* 44a)

It is taught in a *Baraita* [Rabbinic source], that Rabbi Natan says: There is no *mitzvah*, however minor, that is written in the Torah, for which there is no reward given in this world; and in the World-to-Come I do not know how much reward is given.

Go and learn from the following incident concerning the *mitzvah* of *tzitzit* [ritual fringes]. incident involving a certain man who was diligent about the *mitzvah* of *tzitzit*. This man heard that there was a prostitute in one of the cities overseas who took four hundred gold coins as her payment. He sent her four hundred gold coins and fixed a time to meet with her. When his time came, he came and sat at the entrance to her house.

The maidservant of that prostitute entered and said to her: That man who sent you four hundred gold coins came and sat at the entrance. She said: Let him enter. He entered. She arranged seven

213

beds for him, six of silver and one of gold. Between each and every one of them there was a ladder made of silver, and the top bed was had a ladder that was made of gold.

She went up and sat naked on the top bed, and he too went up in order to sit naked facing her. In the meantime, his four *tzitzit* came and slapped him on his face. He dropped down and sat himself on the ground, and she also dropped down and sat on the ground. She said to him: I take an oath by the Roman Capitol that I will not allow you to go until you tell me what defect you saw in me.

He said to her: I take an oath by the Temple service that I never saw a woman as beautiful as you. But there is one *mitzvah* that the Lord, our God, commanded us, and its name is *tzitzit*, and in the passage where it is commanded, it is written twice: "I am the Lord your God" (Numbers 15:41). The doubling of this phrase indicates: I am the one who will punish those who transgress My *mitzvot*, and I am the one who will reward those who fulfill them. Now, said the man, the four sets of *tzitzit* appeared to me as if they were four witnesses who will testify against me.

She said to him: I will not allow you to go until you tell me: What is your name, and what is the name of your city, and what is the name of your teacher, and what is the name of the study hall in which you studied Torah? He wrote the information and placed it in her hand.

She arose and divided all of her property, giving one-third to the government, one-third to the poor, and she took one-third with her in her possession, in addition to those beds of gold and silver.

She came to the study hall of Rabbi Ḥiyya and said to him: My teacher, have your students instruct me and have them make me a convert. Rabbi Ḥiyya said to her: My daughter, perhaps you set your sights on one of the students and that is why you want to convert? She took the note the student had given her from her hand and gave it to Rabbi Ḥiyya. He [converted her and] said to her: Go take possession of your purchase.

Those beds that she had arranged for him in a prohibited fashion, she now arranged for him in a permitted fashion. This is the reward given to him in this world, and with regard to the World-to-Come, I do not know how much reward he will be given.

תניא א"ר נתן אין לך כל מצוה קלה שכתובה בתורה שאין מתן שכרה בעה"ז ולעה"ב איני יודע כמה צא ולמד ממצות ציצית. מעשה באדם אחד שהיה זהיר במצות ציצית שמע שיש זונה בכרכי הים שנוטלת ד' מאות זהובים בשכרה שיגר לה ארבע מאות זהובים וקבע לה זמן כשהגיע זמנו בא וישב על הפתח. נכנסה שפחתה ואמרה לה אותו אדם ששיגר ליך ד' מאות זהובים בא וישב על הפתח אמרה היא יכנס נכנס הציעה לו ז' מטות שש של כסף ואחת של זהב ובין כל אחת ואחת סולם של כסף ועליונה של זהב. עלתה וישבה על גבי עליונה כשהיא ערומה ואף הוא עלה לישב ערום כנגדה באו ד' ציציותיו וטפחו לו על פניו נשמט וישב לו ע"ג קרקע ואף היא נשמטה וישבה ע"ג קרקע אמרה לו גפה של רומי שאיני מניחתך עד שתאמר לי מה מום ראית בי. אמר לה העבודה

שלא ראיתי אשה יפה כמותך אלא מצוה אחת
ציונו ה׳ אלהינו וציצית שמה וכתיב בה (במדבר טו,
מא) אני ה׳ אלהיכם שתי פעמים אני הוא שעתיד
ליפרע ואני הוא שעתיד לשלם שכר עכשיו נדמו עלי
כד׳ עדים. אמרה לו איני מניחך עד שתאמר לי מה
שמך ומה שם עירך ומה שם רבך ומה שם מדרשך
שאתה למד בו תורה כתב ונתן בידה. עמדה
וחילקה כל נכסיה שליש למלכות ושליש לעניים
ושליש נטלה בידה חוץ מאותן מצעות. ובאת לבית
מדרשו של ר׳ חייא אמרה לו רבי צוה עלי ויעשוני
גיורת אמר לה בתי שמא עיניך נתת באחד מן
התלמידים הוציאה כתב מידה ונתנה לו אמר לה
לכי זכי במקחך. אותן מצעות שהציעה לו באיסור
הציעה לו בהיתר זה מתן שכרו בעה״ז ולעה״ב איני
יודע כמה.

(Talmud *Bekhorot* 8a)

All animals mate face to back
except for three who mate
face to face. These are fish,
humans, and snakes. Why
these three. When Rabbi
Dimi came from the West, he
said because God's presence
dwells between them.

הכל משמשין פנים
כנגד עורף חוץ
משלשה שמשמשין
פנים כנגד פנים ואלו
הן דג ואדם ונחש.
ומ״ש הני תלתא כי
אתא רב דימי אמרי
במערבא הואיל
ודיברה עמהם שכינה.

Chapter 3 The Fake ID

(Talmud *Yebamot* 63b)

Ben Azai said, [Those who have no children] is as if they have spilled blood and diminished the Divine Image, as it says Be Fruitful and Multiply. [His students} said to Ben Azai, There are those who interpret well and do well, those who do well but do not interpret well. But you interpret well but do not do well [for he never married nor had children.] Ben Azai said to them, What can I do? My soul is drawn to the Torah. The world must be maintained by others.

(
בֶּן עַזַּאי אוֹמֵר : כְּאִילּוּ
שׁוֹפֵךְ דָּמִים וּמְמַעֵט
הַדְּמוּת, שֶׁנֶּאֱמַר :
״וְאַתֶּם פְּרוּ וּרְבוּ״.
אָמְרוּ לוֹ לְבֶן עַזַּאי : יֵשׁ
נָאֶה דּוֹרֵשׁ וְנָאֶה
מְקַיֵּים, נָאֶה מְקַיֵּים
וְאֵין נָאֶה דּוֹרֵשׁ, וְאַתָּה
נָאֶה דּוֹרֵשׁ, וְאֵין נָאֶה
מְקַיֵּים. אָמַר לָהֶן בֶּן
עַזַּאי : וּמָה אֶעֱשֶׂה
שֶׁנַּפְשִׁי חָשְׁקָה בַּתּוֹרָה,
אֶפְשָׁר לָעוֹלָם
שֶׁיִּתְקַיֵּים עַל יְדֵי
אֲחֵרִים.

(Mishnah *Avot* 4:1)

Ben Zoma said… Who is strong? Whoever can control their urges.

בֶּן זוֹמָא אוֹמֵר, ... אֵיזֶהוּ גִבּוֹר, הַכּוֹבֵשׁ אֶת יִצְרוֹ.

Chapter 4 Second Class The Evil Inclination

(Genesis 2:7)

And the Lord God formed man of the dust of the ground and breathed into his nostrils the breath of life; and man became a living soul.

וַיִּיצֶר יְהֹוָה אֱלֹהִים
אֶת־הָאָדָם עָפָר מִן־
הָאֲדָמָה וַיִּפַּח בְּאַפָּיו
נִשְׁמַת חַיִּים וַיְהִי
הָאָדָם לְנֶפֶשׁ חַיָּה ׃

(Genesis 2:19)

And out of the ground the Lord God formed every beast of the field, and every bird of the air; and brought them to Adam to see what he would call them; and whatever Adam called every living creature, that was its name.

וַיִּצֶר יְהֹוָה אֱלֹהִים מִן־
הָאֲדָמָה כָּל־חַיַּת הַשָּׂדֶה
וְאֵת כָּל־עוֹף הַשָּׁמַיִם
וַיָּבֵא אֶל־הָאָדָם לִרְאוֹת
מַה־יִּקְרָא־לוֹ וְכֹל אֲשֶׁר
יִקְרָא־לוֹ הָאָדָם נֶפֶשׁ
חַיָּה הוּא שְׁמוֹ ׃

(Talmud *Berakhot* 61a)

Rav Naḥman bar Rav Ḥisda said, What is the meaning of that which is written: "Then the Lord God formed [*vayyitzer*] man" (Genesis 2:7), with a double *yod*? This double *yod* alludes to that fact that the Holy One, Blessed be He, created two inclinations; one a good inclination and one an evil inclination.

דָּרַשׁ רַב נַחְמָן בַּר רַב חִסְדָּא : מַאי דִּכְתִיב ״וַיִּיצֶר ה׳ אֱלֹהִים אֶת הָאָדָם״ בִּשְׁנֵי יוֹדִין? שְׁנֵי יְצָרִים בָּרָא הַקָּדוֹשׁ בָּרוּךְ הוּא, אֶחָד יֵצֶר טוֹב וְאֶחָד יֵצֶר רָע.

(*Bereishit Rabbah* 9:7)

If not for the evil inclination, no man would build a house, marry a wife, have a child, or conduct business.

שאלולי יצר הרע, לא בנה אדם בית, ולא נשא אשה, ולא הוליד, ולא נשא ונת

(Talmud *Yoma* 69b)
They imprisoned it [the evil inclination] for three days, looked for a fresh egg throughout the land of Israel, but could not find one.

חַבְשׁוּהוּ תְּלָתָא יוֹמֵי, וּבָעוּ בֵּיעֲתָא בַּת יוֹמָא בְּכָל אֶרֶץ יִשְׂרָאֵל וְלָא אִשְׁתְּכַח.

(Talmud *Sanhedrin* 107a)

Rav Yehuda says that Rav says: A person should never bring himself to undergo an ordeal, as David, king of Israel, brought himself to undergo an ordeal and failed. David said before God: Master of the Universe, for what reason does one say in prayer: God of Abraham, God of Isaac, and God of Jacob, and one does not say: God of David? God said to David: They have undergone ordeals before Me, and you have not undergone an ordeal before Me. David said before Him: Examine me and subject me to an ordeal, as it is stated: "Examine me, Lord, and subject me to an ordeal; try my kidneys and my heart" (Psalms 26:2). God said to him: I will subject you to an ordeal, and I will perform a matter for you that I did not perform for the Patriarchs, as for them, I did not inform them of the nature of the ordeal, while I am informing you that I will subject you to an ordeal involving a matter of a married woman, with whom relations are forbidden. Immediately, it is written: "And it came to pass one evening that David rose from his bed [and saw Bathsheba]." (II Samuel 11:2).

אמר רב יהודה אמר רב לעולם אל יביא אדם עצמו
לידי נסיון שהרי דוד מלך ישראל הביא עצמו לידי
נסיון ונכשל אמר לפניו רבש״ע מפני מה אומרים
אלהי אברהם אלהי יצחק ואלהי יעקב ואין
אומרים אלהי דוד אמר אינהו מינסו לי ואת לא
מינסית לי אמר לפניו רבש״ע בחנני ונסני שנאמר
(תהלים כו, ב) בחנני ה׳ ונסני וגו׳ אמר מינסנא לך
ועבידנא מילתא בהדך דלדידהו לא הודעתינהו
ואילו אנא קא מודענא לך דמנסינא לך בדבר ערוה
מיד (שמואל ב יא, ב) ויהי לעת הערב ויקם דוד
מעל משכבו וגו׳

(Talmud *Sukkah* 52a)

Abaye once heard a certain man say to a certain woman: Let us rise early and go on the road. Upon hearing this, Abaye said to himself: I will go and accompany them and prevent them from violating a prohibition. He went after them for a distance of three parasangs in a marsh among the reeds, while they walked on the road, and they did not engage in any wrongful activity. When they were taking leave of each other, he heard that they were saying: We traveled a long distance together, and the company was pleasant company. Abaye said: In that situation, I would not have been able to restrain himself from sinning. leaned against the doorpost, thinking and feeling regret. A certain Elder came and taught him: the greater the man, the greater the inclination.

כִּי הָא דְּאַבַּיֵי שַׁמְעֵיהּ
לְהַהוּא גַּבְרָא דְּקָאָמַר
לְהַהִיא אִתְּתָא : נַקְדֵּים
וְנֵיזִיל בְּאוֹרְחָא. אֲמַר :
אֵיזִיל אַפְרְשִׁינְהוּ
מֵאִיסּוּרָא. אֲזַל
בָּתְרַיְיהוּ תְּלָתָא פַּרְסֵי
בְּאַגְמָא. כִּי הֲווֹ פָּרְשִׁי
מֵהֲדָדֵי, שַׁמְעִינְהוּ דְּקָא
אָמְרִי : אוֹרְחִין
רַחִיקָא, וְצַוְותִּין
בְּסִימָא. אֲמַר אַבַּיֵי : אִי
מַאן דְּסָנֵי לִי הֲוָה, לָא
הֲוָה מָצֵי לְאוֹקוֹמֵי
נַפְשֵׁיהּ. אֲזַל תְּלָא
נַפְשֵׁיהּ בְּעִיבּוּרָא דְּדָשָׁא
וּמִצְטַעֵר. אֲתָא הָהוּא
סָבָא, תְּנָא לֵיהּ : כָּל
הַגָּדוֹל מֵחֲבֵירוֹ יִצְרוֹ
גָּדוֹל הֵימֶנּוּ.

Chapter 6 Third Class Covering Nakedness

(Genesis 2:25)

The two of them were naked and his wife, yet they felt no shame.

וַיִּהְיוּ שְׁנֵיהֶם֙ עֲרוּמִּ֔ים הָֽאָדָ֖ם וְאִשְׁתּ֑וֹ וְלֹ֖א יִתְבֹּשָֽׁשׁוּ׃

(Genesis 3:7)

Then the eyes of both of them were opened and they perceived that they were naked; and they sewed together fig leaves and made themselves loincloths.

וַתִּפָּקַ֙חְנָה֙ עֵינֵ֣י שְׁנֵיהֶ֔ם וַיֵּ֣דְע֔וּ כִּ֥י עֵֽירֻמִּ֖ם הֵ֑ם וַֽיִּתְפְּרוּ֙ עֲלֵ֣ה תְאֵנָ֔ה וַיַּעֲשׂ֥וּ לָהֶ֖ם חֲגֹרֹֽת׃

(Genesis 3:21)

The Lord God made garments of skins for Adam and his wife, and clothed them.

וַיַּ֩עַשׂ֩ יְהֹוָ֨ה אֱלֹהִ֜ים לְאָדָ֧ם וּלְאִשְׁתּ֛וֹ כָּתְנ֥וֹת ע֖וֹר וַיַּלְבִּשֵֽׁם׃

(Talmud *Sanhedrin* 74a)

Rabbi Yoḥanan says in the name of Rabbi Shimon ben Yehotzadak: The Sages concluded in the upper story of the house of Nitza in the city of Lod: With regard to all other transgressions in the Torah, if a person is told: Transgress this prohibition and you will not be killed, he may transgress that prohibition and not be killed. This is the *halakha* concerning all prohibitions except for those of idol worship, forbidden sexual relations (*gilui arayot*), and bloodshed. Concerning those prohibitions, one must allow himself to be killed rather than transgress them.

אי״ר יוחנן משום ר״ש בן יהוצדק נימנו וגמרו בעליית בית נתזה בלוד כל עבירות שבתורה אם אומרין לאדם עבור ואל תהרג יעבור ואל יהרג חוץ מעבודת כוכבים וגילוי עריות ושפיכות דמים.

(Leviticus 18;7)

Your father's nakedness, that is, the nakedness of your mother, you shall not uncover; she is your mother—you shall not uncover her nakedness.

עֶרְוַת אָבִיךָ וְעֶרְוַת אִמְּךָ לֹא תְגַלֵּה אִמְּךָ הִוא לֹא תְגַלֵּה עֶרְוָתָהּ׃

(Talmud *Berakhot* 24a)

Rav Ḥisda said: Even a woman's exposed leg is considered nakedness, as it is stated: "Uncover the leg and pass through the rivers" (Isaiah 47:2), and it is written in the following verse: "Your nakedness shall be revealed and your shame shall be seen" (Isaiah 47:3). Shmuel further stated: A woman's singing voice is considered nakedness, as it is stated: "Sweet is your voice and your countenance is alluring" (Song of Songs 2:14). Similarly, Rav Sheshet stated: Even a woman's hair is considered nakedness, as it is written: "Your hair is like a flock of goats, trailing down from Mount Gilead"

(Song of Songs 4:1).

אָמַר רַב חִסְדָּא: שׁוֹק בָּאִשָּׁה עֶרְוָה, שֶׁנֶּאֱמַר: ״גַּלִּי שׁוֹק עִבְרִי נְהָרוֹת״, וּכְתִיב: ״תִּגָּל עֶרְוָתֵךְ וְגַם תֵּרָאֶה חֶרְפָּתֵךְ״. אָמַר שְׁמוּאֵל: קוֹל בָּאִשָּׁה עֶרְוָה, שֶׁנֶּאֱמַר: ״כִּי קוֹלֵךְ עָרֵב וּמַרְאֵךְ נָאוֶה״. אָמַר רַב שֵׁשֶׁת: שֵׂעָר בָּאִשָּׁה עֶרְוָה, שֶׁנֶּאֱמַר: ״שַׂעְרֵךְ כְּעֵדֶר הָעִזִּים״.

Chapter 7 The Hotel Room

(Genesis 3:16)

And to the woman [God] said, I will greatly expand your hard labor—and your pregnancies; In hardship shall you bear children. Yet your urge shall be for your husband and he shall rule over you.

אֶל־הָאִשָּׁה אָמַר הַרְבָּה
אַרְבֶּה עִצְּבוֹנֵךְ וְהֵרֹנֵךְ
בְּעֶצֶב תֵּלְדִי בָנִים וְאֶל־
אִישֵׁךְ תְּשׁוּקָתֵךְ וְהוּא
יִמְשָׁל־בָּךְ :

(Genesis 3:19)

By the sweat of your brow shall you get bread to eat, Until you return to the ground— For from it you were taken. For dust you are, and to dust you shall return.

בְּזֵעַת אַפֶּיךָ תֹּאכַל לֶחֶם
עַד שׁוּבְךָ אֶל־הָאֲדָמָה
כִּי מִמֶּנָּה לֻקָּחְתָּ כִּי־עָפָר
אַתָּה וְאֶל־עָפָר תָּשׁוּב :

Chapter 8 Fourth Class Privacy

(Numbers 24:5)

How goodly are your tents O
Jacob, your dwelling places O
Israel.

מַה־טֹּבוּ אֹהָלֶיךָ
יַעֲקֹב מִשְׁכְּנֹתֶיךָ
יִשְׂרָאֵל:

(Rashi on Numbers 24:5)

How goodly are your tents.
He saw the openings, that not
one faced another one.

מה טבו אהליך. עַל
שֶׁרָאָה פִּתְחֵיהֶם שֶׁאֵינָן
מְכֻוָּנִין זֶה מוּל זֶה:

(Shulchan Aruch, *Eben HaEzra* 22:2)

a forbidden sexual partner.

After the episode of Amnon
and Tamar, David and his
court forbade seclusion with
an unmarried woman. Even if
she is not forbidden as an
ervah (person with whom
sexual relations are
forbidden), it is still
considered as seclusion with

כשאירע מעשה אמנון
ותמר גזר דוד ובית
דינו על ייחוד פנויה
ואע״פ שאינה ערוה
בכלל ייחוד עריות
היא.

227

Chapter 9 *The Gay Bar*

(final *vidui* – confessional, version in *Shulchan Aruch Yoreh Deah* 338:2)

I confess before Thee O Lord, my God and the God of my fathers, that my healing and my death are in your hand. May it be Thy will, to heal me completely, and if I die, my death should be an expiation for all sins, wrongs and rebellious acts which I have committed sinfully, wrongfully and rebelliously before Thee, and grant me a share in Paradise, and favor me with the world to come which is stored away for the Righteous.

מודה אני לפניך ה'
אלהי ואלהי אבותי
שרפואתי ומיתתי
בידך יהי רצון מלפניך
שתרפאני רפואה
שלימה ואם אמות
תהא מיתתי כפרה על
כל חטאים ועונות
ופשעים שחטאתי
ושעויתי ושפשעתי
לפניך ותן חלקי בגן
עדן וזכני לעוה"ב
הצפון לצדיקים.

Chapter 10 Fifth Class Sex That Hurts

(Deuteronomy 10:19).

Love the stranger, for you were strangers in the land of Egypt.

וַאֲהַבְתֶּם אֶת־הַגֵּר כִּי־גֵרִים הֱיִיתֶם בְּאֶרֶץ מִצְרָיִם

(Talmud *Eruvin* 100b)

Rami bar Ḥama said that Rav Asi said: It is prohibited for a man to force his wife in the conjugal mitzva, i.e., sexual relations, as it is stated: "And he who hastens with his feet sins" (Proverbs 19:2).

וְאָמַר רָמֵי בַּר חָמָא אָמַר רַב אַסִי: אָסוּר לְאָדָם שֶׁיָּכוֹף אִשְׁתּוֹ לִדְבַר מִצְוָה, שֶׁנֶּאֱמַר: "וְאָץ בְּרַגְלַיִם חוֹטֵא".

(Talmud *Berakhot* 10a)

There were these hooligans in Rabbi Meir's neighborhood who caused him a great deal of anguish. Rabbi Meir prayed for God that they should die. Rabbi Meir's wife, Berurya, said to him: What is your thinking? On what basis do you pray for the death of these hooligans? Do you base yourself on the verse, as it is written: "Let sins cease from the land" (Psalms 104:35), which you interpret to mean that the world would be better if the wicked were destroyed? But is it written, let sinners cease?" Let sins cease, is written. Moreover, go to the end of the verse, where it says: "And the wicked will be no more." If, as you suggest, transgressions shall cease refers to the demise of the evildoers, how is it possible that the wicked will be no more, i.e., that they will no longer be evil? Rather, pray for God to have mercy on them, that they should repent. He prayed for God to have mercy on them, and they repented.

הָנְהוּ בִּרְיוֹנֵי דַּהֲווֹ
בְּשִׁבְבוּתֵיהּ דְּרַבִּי מֵאִיר
וַהֲווֹ קָא מְצַעֲרוּ לֵיהּ
טוּבָא. הֲוָה קָא בָּעֵי
רַבִּי מֵאִיר רַחֲמֵי
עֲלַוְיְהוּ כִּי הֵיכִי
דְּלֵימוּתוּ. אָמְרָה לֵיהּ
בְּרוּרְיָא דְּבֵיתְהוּ: מַאי
דַּעְתָּךְ מִשּׁוּם דִּכְתִיב
"יִתַּמּוּ חַטָּאִים", מִי
כְּתִיב "חוֹטְאִים"?
"חַטָּאִים" כְּתִיב.
וְעוֹד, שְׁפֵיל לְסֵיפֵיהּ
דִּקְרָא "וּרְשָׁעִים עוֹד
אֵינָם", כֵּיוָן דְּ"יִתַּמּוּ
חַטָּאִים" "וּרְשָׁעִים עוֹד
אֵינָם"? אֶלָּא בְּעִי רַחֲמֵי
עֲלַוְיְהוּ דְּלַהֲדְרוּ
בִּתְשׁוּבָה, "וּרְשָׁעִים
עוֹד אֵינָם". בְּעָא רַחֲמֵי
עֲלַוְיְהוּ, וַהֲדְרוּ
בִּתְשׁוּבָה.

(Genesis 19:30 – 36)

And Lot went up out of Zoar, and lived in the mountain, and his two daughters with him; for he feared to live in Zoar; and he lived in a cave, he and his two daughters.   And the firstborn said to the younger, Our father is old, and there is not a man on earth to come in to us after the manner of all the earth;   Come, let us make our father drink wine, and we will lie with him, that we may preserve seed of our father.   And they made their father drink wine that night; and the firstborn went in, and lay with her father; and he perceived not when she lay down, nor when she arose.   And it came to pass on the next day, that the firstborn said to the younger, Behold, I lay last night with my father; let us make him drink wine this night also; and you go in, and lie with him, that we may preserve seed of our father. And they made their father drink wine that night also; and the younger arose, and lay with him; and he perceived not when she lay down, nor when she arose. Thus were both the daughters of Lot with child by their father.

ל וַיַּ֩עַל֩ ל֨וֹט מִצּ֜וֹעַר וַיֵּ֣שֶׁב בָּהָ֗ר וּשְׁתֵּ֤י בְנֹתָיו֙ עִמּ֔וֹ כִּ֥י
יָרֵ֖א לָשֶׁ֣בֶת בְּצ֑וֹעַר וַיֵּ֙שֶׁב֙ בַּמְּעָרָ֔ה ה֖וּא וּשְׁתֵּ֥י בְנֹתָֽיו׃
לא וַתֹּ֧אמֶר הַבְּכִירָ֛ה אֶל־הַצְּעִירָ֖ה אָבִ֣ינוּ זָקֵ֑ן וְאִ֤ישׁ
אֵ֣ין בָּאָ֗רֶץ לָב֤וֹא עָלֵ֙ינוּ֙ כְּדֶ֖רֶךְ כָּל־הָאָֽרֶץ׃ לב לְכָ֞ה
נַשְׁקֶ֤ה אֶת־אָבִ֙ינוּ֙ יַ֔יִן וְנִשְׁכְּבָ֖ה עִמּ֑וֹ וּנְחַיֶּ֥ה מֵאָבִ֖ינוּ
זָֽרַע׃ לג וַתַּשְׁקֶ֧יןָ אֶת־אֲבִיהֶ֛ן יַ֖יִן בַּלַּ֣יְלָה ה֑וּא וַתָּבֹ֤א
הַבְּכִירָה֙ וַתִּשְׁכַּ֣ב אֶת־אָבִ֔יהָ וְלֹֽא־יָדַ֥ע בְּשִׁכְבָ֖הּ
וּבְקוּמָֽהּ׃ לד וַֽיְהִי֙ מִֽמָּחֳרָ֔ת וַתֹּ֤אמֶר הַבְּכִירָה֙ אֶל־
הַצְּעִירָ֔ה הֵן־שָׁכַ֥בְתִּי אֶ֖מֶשׁ אֶת־אָבִ֑י נַשְׁקֶ֨נּוּ יַ֜יִן גַּם־
הַלַּ֗יְלָה וּבֹ֙אִי֙ שִׁכְבִ֣י עִמּ֔וֹ וּנְחַיֶּ֥ה מֵאָבִ֖ינוּ זָֽרַע׃
לה וַתַּשְׁקֶ֜יןָ גַּ֣ם בַּלַּ֧יְלָה הַה֛וּא אֶת־אֲבִיהֶ֖ן יָ֑יִן וַתָּ֤קָם
הַצְּעִירָה֙ וַתִּשְׁכַּ֣ב עִמּ֔וֹ וְלֹֽא־יָדַ֥ע בְּשִׁכְבָ֖הּ וּבְקֻמָֽהּ׃
לו וַֽתַּהֲרֶ֛יןָ שְׁתֵּ֥י בְנֽוֹת־ל֖וֹט מֵאֲבִיהֶֽן׃

(Exodus 20: 13)

Do not commit adultery.

לֹא תִּנְאָף

(Deuteronomy 23:3)

Someone misbegotten (a mamzer) shall not enter into the community of the Lord, for ten generations he may not come into the congregation of the Lord.

לֹא־יָבֹא מַמְזֵר בִּקְהַל
יְהֹוָה גַּם דּוֹר עֲשִׂירִי
לֹא־יָבֹא לוֹ בִּקְהַל
יְהֹוָה:

(Genesis 39:7)

After a time, his master's wife cast her eyes upon Joseph and said, Lie with me. (Genesis 39:7)

וַיְהִי אַחַר הַדְּבָרִים
הָאֵלֶּה וַתִּשָּׂא אֵשֶׁת־
אֲדֹנָיו אֶת־עֵינֶיהָ אֶל־
יוֹסֵף וַתֹּאמֶר שִׁכְבָה
עִמִּי:

Chapter 11 God Protects the Innocent

(Joshua 2:1)

Joshua son of Nun secretly sent two spies from Shittim, saying, Go, reconnoiter the region of Jericho. So they set out, and they came to the house of a harlot named Rahab and lodged there.

וַיִּשְׁלַח יְהוֹשֻׁעַ־בִּן־נוּן
מִן־הַשִּׁטִּים שְׁנַיִם־
אֲנָשִׁים מְרַגְּלִים חֶרֶשׁ
לֵאמֹר לְכוּ רְאוּ אֶת־
הָאָרֶץ וְאֶת־יְרִיחוֹ וַיֵּלְכוּ
וַיָּבֹאוּ בֵּית־אִשָּׁה זוֹנָה
וּשְׁמָהּ רָחָב וַיִּשְׁכְּבוּ־
שָׁמָּה :

(Talmud *Megillah* 14b)

Eight prophets, who were also priests, descended from Rahab the prostitute, and they are: Neriah; his son Baruch; Seraiah; Mahseiah; Jeremiah; his father, Hilkiah; Jeremiah's cousin Hanamel; and Hanamel's father, Shallum. Rabbi Yehuda said: So too, Huldah the prophetess was a descendant of Rahab the prostitute.

שְׁמוֹנָה נְבִיאִים וְהֵם
כֹּהֲנִים יָצְאוּ מֵרָחָב
הַזּוֹנָה, וְאֵלּוּ הֵן : נֵרִיָּה,
בָּרוּךְ, וּשְׂרָיָה, מַחְסֵיָה,
יִרְמְיָה, חִלְקִיָּה,
חֲנַמְאֵל, וְשַׁלּוּם. רַבִּי
יְהוּדָה אוֹמֵר : אַף
חֻלְדָּה הַנְּבִיאָה מִבְּנֵי
בָנֶיהָ שֶׁל רָחָב הַזּוֹנָה
הָיְתָה.

(Psalms 116:6)

God protects the innocent, I was brought low and He saved me.

שֹׁמֵר פְּתָאיִם יְהֹוָה דַּלּוֹתִי וְלִי יְהוֹשִׁיעַ:

(Genesis 38:9)

But Onan, knowing that the offspring would not count as his whenever he joined with his brother's wife, so as not to provide offspring for his brother, so he wasted his seed on the ground.

וַיֵּדַע אוֹנָן כִּי לֹא לוֹ
יִהְיֶה הַזָּרַע וְהָיָה אִם־
בָּא אֶל־אֵשֶׁת אָחִיו
וְשִׁחֵת אַרְצָה לְבִלְתִּי
נְתָן־זֶרַע לְאָחִיו:

Chapter 12 Sixth Class Non-Marital Sex

(Talmud *Sanhedrin* 75a)

Rav Yehuda says that Rav says: There was an incident involving a certain man who set his eyes upon a certain woman and passion rose in his heart, to the point that he became deathly ill. And they came and asked doctors what was to be done with him. And the doctors said: He will have no cure until she engages in sexual intercourse with him. The Sages said: Let him die, but she may not engage in sexual intercourse with him. The doctors said: She should at least stand naked before him. The Sages said: Let him die, but she may not stand naked before him. The doctors suggested: The woman should at least converse with him behind a fence in a secluded area.. The Sages insisted: Let him die, but she may not converse with him behind a fence.

Rabbi Ya'akov bar Idi and Rabbi Shmuel bar Naḥmani disagree about this issue. One of them says: The woman in question was a married woman, and the other one says: She was unmarried. Granted, according to the one who says that she was a married woman, the matter is properly understood. But according to the one who says that she was unmarried, what is the reason for all this opposition? Rav Pappa says: This is due to the potential harm to the family name. Rav Aḥa, son of Rav Ika, says: This is so that the daughters of Israel should not be promiscuous with regard to forbidden sexual relations.

But if the woman was unmarried, let the man marry her. His mind would not have been eased by marriage, in accordance with the statement of Rabbi Yitzḥak. As Rabbi Yitzḥak says: Since the day the Temple was destroyed, sexual pleasure was taken away from those who engage in permitted intercourse and given to transgressors, as it is stated: *Stolen waters are sweet, and bread eaten in secret is pleasant* (Proverbs 9:17).

אמר רב יהודה אמר רב מעשה באדם אחד שנתן עיניו באשה אחת והעלה לבו טינא ובאו ושאלו לרופאים ואמרו אין לו תקנה עד שתבעל אמרו חכמים ימות ואל תבעל לו תעמוד לפניו ערומה ימות ואל תעמוד לפניו ערומה תספר עמו מאחורי הגדר ימות ולא תספר עמו מאחורי הגדר. פליגי בה ר' יעקב בר אידי ור' שמואל בר נחמני חד אמר אשת איש היתה וחד אמר פנויה היתה בשלמא למאן דאמר אשת איש היתה שפיר אלא למ"ד פנויה היתה מאי כולי האי. רב פפא אמר משום פגם משפחה רב אחא בריה דרב איקא אמר כדי שלא יהו בנות ישראל פרוצות בעריות. ולינסבה מינסב לא מייתבה דעתיה כדר' יצחק דא"ר יצחק מיום שחרב בית המקדש ניטלה טעם ביאה וניתנה לעוברי עבירה שנאמר (משלי ט, יז) מים גנובים ימתקו ולחם סתרים ינעם :

(Genesis 26:8)

When some time had passed, Abimelech king of the Philistines, looking out of the window, saw Isaac playing with his wife Rebekah.

יְהִ֗י כִּ֣י אָֽרְכוּ־ל֥וֹ שָׁם֙ הַיָּמִ֔ים וַיַּשְׁקֵ֗ף אֲבִימֶ֙לֶךְ֙ מֶ֣לֶךְ פְּלִשְׁתִּ֔ים בְּעַ֖ד הַֽחַלּ֑וֹן וַיַּ֗רְא וְהִנֵּ֤ה יִצְחָק֙ מְצַחֵ֔ק אֵ֖ת רִבְקָ֥ה אִשְׁתּֽוֹ:

Chapter 13 Sex and Kabbalah

(*Avot* 5:16)

All love that depends on a something, [when the] thing ceases, [the] love ceases; and [all love] that does not depend on anything, will never cease. What is an example of love that depended on a something? Such was the love of Amnon for Tamar. And what is an example of love that did not depend on anything? Such was the love of David and Jonathan.

כָּל אַהֲבָה שֶׁהִיא תְלוּיָה בְדָבָר, בָּטֵל דָּבָר, בְּטֵלָה אַהֲבָה. וְשֶׁאֵינָהּ תְּלוּיָה בְדָבָר, אֵינָהּ בְּטֵלָה לְעוֹלָם. אֵיזוֹ הִיא אַהֲבָה הַתְּלוּיָה בְדָבָר, זוֹ אַהֲבַת אַמְנוֹן וְתָמָר. וְשֶׁאֵינָהּ תְּלוּיָה בְדָבָר, זוֹ אַהֲבַת דָּוִד וִיהוֹנָתָן:

(*Siddur* [prayerbook], *Nusach Sefard*)

In order to unite the Holy One Blessed be He and His *Shekhinah*, in awe and in love, in order to reunite the letters of God's as One in the name of all Israel …

לְשֵׁם יְחוּד קוּדְשָׁא בְּרִיךְ הוּא וּשְׁכִינְתֵּהּ, בִּדְחִילוּ וּרְחִימוּ לְיַחֵד שֵׁם יֽ"ה בו"ה בְּיִחוּדָא שְׁלִים בְּשֵׁם כָּל יִשְׂרָאֵל.

Chapter 14 Seventh Class Climbing the Ladder

(Jerusalem Talmud, *Kiddushin* 4:12)

Hizkiya and Rabbi Kohen said in the name of Rav, In the future every person will have to give an accounting and everything [legitimate pleasure] their eye saw but they did not eat.

רְבִי חִזְקִיָה רְבִי כֹהֵן בְּשֵׁם רַב. עָתִיד אָדָם לִיתֵּן דִין וְחֶשְׁבּוֹן עַל כָּל־מַה שֶׁרָאֲת עֵינוֹ וְלֹא אָכַל.

(Talmud, *Yebamot* 12b)

Rabbi Bibi taught before Rav Hahman, three women use a *mokh* (absorbent birth control pad), a child, a pregnant woman, and a nursing woman. A child, less she become pregnant and die. A pregnant woman, less her fetus become deformed like a sandal fish, a nursing woman lest she wean her child too soon and it dies.

תָּנֵי רַב בִּיבִי קַמֵּיה דְּרַב נַחְמָן, שָׁלֹש נָשִׁים מְשַׁמְּשׁוֹת בְּמוֹךְ : קְטַנָּה, מְעוּבֶּרֶת, וּמְנִיקָה. קְטַנָּה שֶׁמָּא תִּתְעַבֵּר וְשֶׁמָּא תָּמוּת. מְעוּבֶּרֶת שֶׁמָּא תַּעֲשֶׂה עוּבָּרָה סַנְדָּל. מְנִיקָה שֶׁמָּא תִּגְמוֹל בְּנָה וְיָמוּת.

239

(Talmud *Yebamot* 65b)

Yehudit, the wife of Rabbi Ḥiyya, had acute birthing pain from these unusual deliveries. She changed her clothes to prevent Rabbi Ḥiyya from recognizing her and came before Rabbi Ḥiyya to ask him a halakhic question. She said: Is a woman commanded to be fruitful and multiply? He said to her: No. She went and drank an infertility potion (cup of roots).

יְהוּדִית, דְּבֵיתְהוּ דְּרַבִּי חִיָּא, הֲוָה לַהּ צַעַר לֵידָה. שַׁנַּאי מָנַהּ, וַאֲתַאי לְקַמֵּיהּ דְּרַבִּי חִיָּא, אֲמַרָה: אִתְּתָא מִפַּקְּדָא אַפְּרִיָּה וּרְבִיָּה? אֲמַר לַהּ: לָא. אֲזַלָא אִשְׁתְּיָא סַמָּא דַעֲקַרְתָּא.

(Talmud *Yebamot* 34b)

For twenty-four months a man may thresh within and winnow without (practice coitus interruptus), these are the words of Rabbi Eliezer. The Sages said to him, this was the practice of Er and Onan.

כָּל עֶשְׂרִים וְאַרְבָּעָה חֹדֶשׁ דָּשׁ מִבִּפְנִים וְזוֹרֶה מִבַּחוּץ, דִּבְרֵי רַבִּי אֱלִיעֶזֶר. אָמְרוּ לוֹ: הֲלָלוּ אֵינוֹ אֶלָּא כְּמַעֲשֵׂה עֵר וְאוֹנָן.

Chapter 15 The Concert

(Yom Kippur *Mahzor*, *Kol Nidre* Service)

With the consent of the Almighty, and consent of this congregation, in a convocation of the heavenly court, and a convocation of the lower court,[3]*The court of man.* we hereby grant permission to pray with transgressors.

עַל דַּעַת הַמָּקוֹם וְעַל דַּעַת הַקָּהָל. בִּישִׁיבָה שֶׁל מַעְלָה וּבִישִׁיבָה שֶׁל מַטָּה. אָנוּ מַתִּירִין לְהִתְפַּלֵּל עִם הָעֲבַרְיָנִים :

(Genesis 48:20)

May God bless you as he blessed Efraim and Manasseh.

יְשִׂמְךָ אֱלֹהִים כְּאֶפְרַיִם וְכִמְנַשֶּׁה

241

Chapter 16 Eighth Class The Marital Bedroom

(Mishnah *Kiddushin* 1:1)

A wife is acquired in three ways … with money, with a document, or through a sexual act.

הָאִשָּׁה נִקְנֵית בְּשָׁלֹש
דְּרָכִים, ... בְּכֶסֶף,
בִּשְׁטָר, וּבְבִיאָה.

(Exodus 21:10)

If he takes another [into the household as his wife], he must not withhold from this one her food, her clothing, or her conjugal rights.

אִם־אַחֶרֶת יִקַּח־לוֹ
שְׁאֵרָהּ כְּסוּתָהּ וְעֹנָתָהּ
לֹא יִגְרָע׃

(Talmud *Pesachim* 72b)

Rava said, A man is obligated to give his wife joy in regard to the mitzvah.

אָמַר רָבָא : חַיָּיב אָדָם
לְשַׂמֵּחַ אִשְׁתּוֹ בִּדְבַר
מִצְוָה.

(Mishnah *Kiddushin* 5:6)

The sexual rights (*onah*) mentioned in the Torah. For men of leisure, every day. For workers, twice a week. For ass drivers, once a week. For camel drivers, once every thirty days. For sailors, once every six months. This is the opinion of Rabbi Eliezer.

הָעוֹנָה הָאֲמוּרָה בַּתּוֹרָה, הַטַּיָּלִין, בְּכָל יוֹם. הַפּוֹעֲלִים, שְׁתַּיִם בַּשַּׁבָּת. הַחַמָּרִים, אַחַת בַּשַּׁבָּת. הַגַּמָּלִים, אַחַת לִשְׁלֹשִׁים יוֹם. הַסַּפָּנִים, אַחַת לְשִׁשָּׁה חֳדָשִׁים, דִּבְרֵי רַבִּי אֱלִיעֶזֶר:

(Talmud *Ketubot* 48a)

Rav Yosef taught, the word *sh'eira* [we translated as "food" but also means flesh] is understood as closeness of flesh, that one should not follow the tradition of the Persians, who have sexual relations while wearing clothing.

תָּנֵי רַב יוֹסֵף: "שְׁאֵרָה" זוֹ קֵרוּב בָּשָׂר, שֶׁלֹּא יִנְהַג בָּהּ מִנְהַג פָּרְסִיִּים שֶׁמְּשַׁמְּשִׁין מִטּוֹתֵיהֶן בִּלְבוּשֵׁיהֶן.

243

(Talmud *Niddah* 17a)

Rav Ḥisda says: It is prohibited for a person to engage in intercourse by day, as it is stated: "And you shall love your fellow as yourself" (Leviticus 19:18). From where is this inferred? Abaye says: If one engages in intercourse by day, perhaps the husband will see some blemish in his wife and she will become repugnant to him. Rav Huna says: Jews are holy, and they do not engage in intercourse by day.

אמר רב חסדא אסור
לו לאדם שישמש
מטתו ביום שנאמר
(ויקרא יט, יח) ואהבת
לרעך כמוך מאי משמע
אמר אביי שמא יראה
בה דבר מגונה ותתגנה
עליו אמר רב הונא
ישראל קדושים הם
ואין משמשין
מטותיהן ביום.

(Leviticus 18:19)

Do not come near a woman during her menstrual period of impurity to uncover her nakedness.

וְאֶל־אִשָּׁה בְּנִדַּת
טֻמְאָתָהּ לֹא תִקְרַב
לְגַלּוֹת עֶרְוָתָהּ :

(Rambam *Mishnah Torah, Isurei Biah* 21:9)

A man is permitted to have sexual relations with his wife in any way he pleases. What he wishes to do with his wife, he may do. He can have sex whenever he pleases and kiss any organs he desires. He can have natural or unnatural sex, provided he does not release seed in vain.

אִשְׁתּוֹ שֶׁל אָדָם מֻתֶּרֶת הִיא לוֹ. לְפִיכָךְ כָּל מַה שֶׁאָדָם רוֹצֶה לַעֲשׂוֹת בְּאִשְׁתּוֹ עוֹשֶׂה. בּוֹעֵל בְּכָל עֵת שֶׁיִּרְצֶה וּמְנַשֵּׁק בְּכָל אֵיבָר וְאֵיבָר שֶׁיִּרְצֶה. [וּבָא עָלֶיהָ כְּדַרְכָּהּ וְשֶׁלֹּא כְּדַרְכָּהּ] וּבִלְבַד שֶׁלֹּא יוֹצִיא שִׁכְבַת זֶרַע לְבַטָּלָה.

(*Tosafot* on Talmud *Yebamot* 34b)

It is not considered like the act of Er and Onan unless it was his intention to destroy seed and he does it regularly. But if it is occasional and it is his desire to come upon his wife in this unnatural way, it is permitted.

דלא חשוב כמעשה ער ואונן אלא כשמתכוין להשחית זרע ורגיל לעשות כן תמיד אבל באקראי בעלמא ומתאוה לבא על אשתו שלא כדרכה שרי.

(Talmud *Niddah* 66a)

Rav Zeira taught, the children of Israel are strict with themselves, that even if they see a spot of blood the size of a mustard seed, they wait for seven clean days.

אמר ר' זירא : בנות ישראל החמירו על עצמן, שאפילו רואות טפת דם כחרדל - יושבות עליה שבעה נקיים.

(Talmud *Niddah* 31b)

Rabbi Meir said, why does the Torah teach a menstrual woman is a state of impurity seven days. If her husband becomes too familiar to her, he might become repulsed by her. She is separated from him seven days, so that she will be as dear to him as on their wedding day.

היה ר"מ אומר : מפני מה אמרה תורה נדה לשבעה - מפני שרגיל בה, וקץ בה, אמרה תורה : תהא טמאה שבעה ימים, כדי שתהא חביבה על בעלה כשעת כניסתה לחופה.

(Talmud *Shabbat* 21b)

The reason for the school of Hillel, one should go up in holiness and not come down in holiness.

טעמא דבית הלל - דמעלין בקדש ואין מורידין.

Chapter 17 The Abortion Clinic

(Exodus 21:22)

When men fight, and one of them pushes a pregnant woman and a miscarriage results, but no other damage ensues, the one responsible shall be fined according as the woman's husband may exact from him, the payment to be based on reckoning.

וְכִי־יִנָּצוּ אֲנָשִׁים וְנָגְפוּ אִשָּׁה הָרָה וְיָצְאוּ יְלָדֶיהָ וְלֹא יִהְיֶה אָסוֹן עָנוֹשׁ יֵעָנֵשׁ כַּאֲשֶׁר יָשִׁית עָלָיו בַּעַל הָאִשָּׁה וְנָתַן בִּפְלִלִים׃

(Numbers 35:31)

You may not accept a ransom for the life of a murderer who is guilty of a capital crime; he must be put to death.

וְלֹא־תִקְחוּ כֹפֶר לְנֶפֶשׁ רֹצֵחַ אֲשֶׁר־הוּא רָשָׁע לָמוּת כִּי־מוֹת יוּמָת׃

(Rashi on Talmud *Sanhedrin* 72b)

The entire time that that it has not gone out into the air of the world, it is not [considered] a soul.

דכל זמן שלא יצא לאויר העולם לאו נפש הוא.

(Mishnah *Oholot* 7:6)

If a woman is having trouble giving birth, they cut up the child in her womb and brings it forth limb by limb, because her life comes before the life of [the child]. But if the greater part has come out, one may not touch it, for one may not set aside one person's life for that of another.

הָאִשָּׁה שֶׁהִיא מַקְשָׁה
לֵילֵד, מְחַתְּכִין אֶת
הַוָּלָד בְּמֵעֶיהָ וּמוֹצִיאִין
אוֹתוֹ אֲבָרִים אֲבָרִים,
מִפְּנֵי שֶׁחַיֶּיהָ קוֹדְמִין
לְחַיָּיו. יָצָא רֻבּוֹ, אֵין
נוֹגְעִין בּוֹ, שֶׁאֵין דּוֹחִין
נֶפֶשׁ מִפְּנֵי נָפֶשׁ.

(Responsa of Rabbi Yehudah L. Perilman, *Or Gadol* 31)

She differs from the ground of the earth in that she need not nurture seed planted in her against her will.

דהקרקע עולם שלה
אינו משועבד להזרע
שנזרע בה שלא
מדעתה.

(Deuteronomy 30:19)

Therefore choose life.

וּבָחַרְתָּ בַּחַיִּים

(Mishnah *Baba Kama* 8:7)

If a man said, "Blind my eye", or "Cut off my hand", or "Break my foot", he [that does so] is liable. [If he added] "On the condition that you will be exempt", he is still liable. [If he said] "Tear my garment", or "Break my jug", he that does so is liable. [If he added] "On the condition that you will be exempt", he is exempt. [If he said], "Do so to so-and-so, on the condition that you will be exempt, he is liable, whether it was [an offense] against his person or his property.

הָאוֹמֵר סַמֵּא אֶת עֵינִי, קְטַע אֶת יָדִי, שְׁבֹר אֶת רַגְלִי, חַיָּב. עַל מְנָת לִפְטֹר, חַיָּב. קְרַע אֶת כְּסוּתִי, שְׁבֹר אֶת כַּדִּי, חַיָּב. עַל מְנָת לִפְטֹר, פָּטוּר. עָשָׂה כֵן לְאִישׁ פְּלוֹנִי, עַל מְנָת לִפְטֹר, חַיָּב, בֵּין בְּגוּפוֹ בֵּין בְּמָמוֹנוֹ.

(Talmud *Yebamot* 69b)

Rav Ḥisda said: She (a priest's daughter who is widowed) immerses and partakes of *teruma* only until forty days after her husband's death, when there is still no reason for concern, as if she is not pregnant then she is not pregnant. And if she is pregnant, until forty days from conception the fetus is merely water.

אמר רב חסדא טובלת
ואוכלת עד ארבעים
דאי לא מיעברא הא
לא מיעברא ואי
מיעברא עד ארבעים
מיא בעלמא היא

Chapter 18 Nineth Class Gay and Jewish

(Leviticus 18:22)

Do not lie with a male as one lies with a woman; it is an abhorrence.

וְאֶת־זָכָ֕ר לֹ֥א תִשְׁכַּ֖ב מִשְׁכְּבֵ֣י אִשָּׁ֑ה תּוֹעֵבָ֖ה הִֽוא׃

(Leviticus 20:13)

If a man lies with a male as one lies with a woman, the two of them have done an abhorrent thing; they shall be put to death—their bloodguilt is upon them.

וְאִ֗ישׁ אֲשֶׁ֨ר יִשְׁכַּ֤ב אֶת־ זָכָר֙ מִשְׁכְּבֵ֣י אִשָּׁ֔ה תּוֹעֵבָ֥ה עָשׂ֖וּ שְׁנֵיהֶ֑ם מ֥וֹת יוּמָ֖תוּ דְּמֵיהֶ֥ם בָּֽם׃

(Rashi on Leviticus 20:13)

'As one lies with a woman.' As if he inserts a makeup brush into a tube.

מַכְנִיס כְּמִכְחוֹל משכבי בִּשְׁפוֹפֶרֶת אשה.

(Talmud *Nedarim* 51a)

Bar Kappara said to Rabbi Yehuda HaNasi at the wedding: What is the meaning of the word *to'eva*, abomination (Leviticus 18:22)? Whatever it was that Rabbi Yehuda HaNasi said to bar Kappara in explanation, claiming that this is the meaning of *to'eva*, bar Kappara refuted it by proving otherwise. Rabbi Yehuda HaNasi said to him: You explain it. Bar Kappara said to him: Let your wife come and pour me a goblet of wine. She came and poured him wine. Bar Kappara then said to Rabbi Yehuda HaNasi: Arise and dance for me, so that I will tell you the meaning of the word: This is what the Merciful One is saying in the Torah in the word *to'eva*: You are straying after it [*to'e ata bah*].

אֲמַר לֵיה בַּר קַפָּרָא
לְרַבִּי מַאי תּוֹעֵבָה כֹּל
דַּאֲמַר לֵיה רַבִּי דְּהָכֵין
הוּא תּוֹעֵבָה פַּרְכַהּ בַּר
קַפָּרָא אֲמַר לֵיה
פָּרְשֵׁיהּ אַתְּ אֲמַר לֵיה
תֵּיתֵי דְּבֵיתְכִי תִּירְמֵי
לִי נַטְלָא אֲתָת רָמְיָא
לֵיה אֲמַר לֵיה לְרַבִּי
קוּם רְקוֹד לִי דְּאֵימַר
לָךְ הָכִי אָמַר רַחֲמָנָא
תּוֹעֵבָה תּוֹעֶה אַתָּה בָּהּ.

(Genesis 19:5)

And they called to Lot, and said to him, Where are the men who came in to you this night? Bring them out to us, that we may know them.

וַיִּקְרְאוּ אֶל־לוֹט וַיֹּאמְרוּ לוֹ אַיֵּה הָאֲנָשִׁים אֲשֶׁר־בָּאוּ אֵלֶיךָ הַלָּיְלָה הוֹצִיאֵם אֵלֵינוּ וְנֵדְעָה אֹתָם :

(Talmud *Yebamot* 76a)

Rav Huna said: Women who rub against one another motivated by sexual desire are unfit to marry into the priesthood, as such conduct renders a woman a *zona*, whom a priest is prohibited from marrying. (The Talmud says that the *halakha* is not in accordance with Rav Huna's opinion.)

אָמַר רַב הוּנָא : נָשִׁים הַמְסוֹלְלוֹת זוֹ בָּזוֹ, פְּסוּלוֹת לַכְּהוּנָה.

RESOURCES

Abortion Rights Planned Parenthood
www.plannedparenthood.org/learn/abortion

Cyberbullying Cyber Civil Rights Initiative www.cyber
civilrights.org

Sex Education Sexuality Information and Education Councill of
the United States www.siecus.org

BIBLIOGRAPHY

Borowitz, Eugene. *Choosing a Sex Ethic.* New York: Schocken Books, 1969.

Bulka, Reuven P. *The Jewish Pleasure Principle.* New York: Human Sciences Press, 1987.

Cohen, Seymour. Translator and Editor, *Epistle of Holiness* by Nachmanides, New York: Ktav, 1976.

Feldman, David. *Marital Relations, Birth Control, and Abortion in Jewish Law.* New York: Schocken Books, 1974.

Friedman, Manis. *Doesn't Anyone Blush Anymore? Reclaiming Intimacy, Modesty, and Sexuality.* San Francisco: Harper Collins, 1990.

Gold, Michael. *Does God Belong in the Bedroom?* Philadelphia: The Jewish Publication Society, 1992.

Goldman, Alan H. "Why Sexual Morality Doesn't Exist." Published in Institute of Art and Issues, https://iai.tv/articles/why-sexual-morality-does-not-exist-auid-1212.

Greenberg, Steven. *Wrestling with God and Men; Homosexuality in the Jewish Tradition*, Madison, WI: University of Wisconsin Press, 2005.

Lamm, Norman. *A Hedge of Roses.* New York: Feldheim Publishers, 1980.

Nagel, Thomas. "Sexual Perversion" in *Moral Questions.* New York: Cambridge University Press, 1979.

Nelson, James. *Between Two Gardens.* New York: Pilgrim Press, 1983.

Perry, Louise. *The Case Against the Sexual Revolution.* Cambridge, UK: Polity Press, 2022.

Ruttenberg, Dana. *The Passionate Torah; Sex and Judaism.* New York: New York University Press, 2009.

ABOUT THE AUTHOR

Rabbi Michael Gold retired from the pulpit of Temple Beth Torah, Tamarac Jewish Center in Tamarac, Florida in 2022, after serving there 32 years. Previously, he served as rabbi of Beth El Congregation in Pittsburgh, Pennsylvania and Congregation Sons of Israel in Upper Nyack, New York. Currently he has a part time position as the rabbi of Temple Beth Shalom in Century Village, Boca Raton, FL.

A native of Los Angeles, Rabbi Gold received his B.A. in mathematics from the University of California in San Diego. The Jewish Theological Seminary ordained him in 1979. He received his PhD in the Public Intellectuals Program at Florida Atlantic University in 2016, with a dissertation on process philosophy and Jewish mysticism. He is an adjunct professor of philosophy and religion at Broward and Miami-Dade Colleges in Florida and Charter Oak College in Connecticut.

Rabbi Gold has lectured throughout the country, in Europe, and in Mexico on sexual ethics, infertility and adoption, love and family, science and spirituality, and finding a mission in life. His articles have appeared in numerous publications, including *Moment, Judaism,* the *Jewish Spectator,* and the *B'nai Brith International Jewish Monthly.* He has developed courses on various spiritual topics for udemy.com. His weekly spiritual message goes to hundreds of readers of all faiths throughout the world.

Rabbi Michael and Evelyn Gold are the parents of three children and one grandchild.

ALSO BY RABBI MICHAEL GOLD

Three Creation Stories; A Rabbi Encounters the Universe (Wipf & Stock) 2018.

The Kabbalah of Love; The Journey of a Soul (Booksurge) 2008.

The Ten Journeys of Life; Walking the Path of Abraham, A Guide to Being Human (Simcha Press) 2007.

*God, Love, Sex, and Family; A Rabbi's Guide for Building Relationships (*Jason Aronson Inc.) 1998.

Does God Belong in the Bedroom? (The Jewish Publication Society) 1992.

And *Hannah Wept; Infertility, Adoption, and the Jewish Couple* (The Jewish Publication Society) 1988.

DISCUSSION GUIDE FOR SMALL GROUPS OR PERSONAL REFLECTION

1. God in the Bedroom – Rabbi Williams tells his wife the Talmudic story of Kahane, who hid under his rabbi's bed while his rabbi made love with his wife. Kahane claims, this too is Torah and he comes to learn. Should the Torah be concerned with what happens in the privacy of the bedroom? To put it more broadly, should religion be concerned with sexual behavior?

2. Humans and Animals – Rabbi Williams emphasizes the difference between humans and animals. For example, most humans have sex face-to-face while most animals mount from the back. Is this important? Another point, most animals only mate when the female is in heat, usually leading to pregnancy. Humans have sex any time of the month. Is this difference relevant?

3. Privacy – Rabbi Williams teaches his students the importance of privacy, emphasizing the Rabbinic tradition that in ancient Israel, the doors of the tents did not face each other. Have we lost our sense of privacy in this age of social media? Is there a limit of what people should post on social media?

4. The Evil Inclination and the Id – Rabbi Williams speaks of the evil inclination, which he identifies with our appetites out of control, particularly our sexual appetite. Sigmund Freud, born Jewish but an atheist, speaks of the id or inner drives, particularly the sexual drive. Is the id the same as the evil inclination? Was Freud influenced by his Jewish upbringing? What is the meaning of Ben Zoma's teaching, "Who is strong? Whoever controls their inclination?"

5. Uncovering Nakedness – Rabbi Williams uses the classical Rabbinic phrase *gilui arayot* – "uncovering nakedness" for forbidden sexual relations. He speaks of covering up a Torah scroll when it is not being used. Is covering something up a way to achieve holiness? When should someone uncover themselves to someone else?

6. Sex and Power – The philosopher Michel Foucault identified sex with power. Rabbi Williams teaches that sex is unethical whenever there is an unequal power relationship between the partners. What is the relationship between sex and power? Is it possible to have a sexual relationship where neither is in a position of power over the other?

7. Non-Marital Sex – Rabbi Williams brings the Talmudic story of a man with an overwhelming desire for a woman, where his life is threatened. The Rabbis forbid sex in this situation, even if it is a threat to the man's life. Why did the Talmud bring this story? Is sex between two consenting, unmarried adults an ethical issue? If it is not, why did the Rabbis forbid it?

8. Man's Obligation and Woman's Right – Rabbi Williams teaches the Biblical law of *onah*, the obligation of a man to have regular sexually relations with his wife. In contemporary thought, we often think of sex as a woman's obligation and a man's right. Why does Judaism reverse this popular view? Why does Judaism obligate a man to provide pleasure to his wife?

9. Natural Law – Nicolas explains to Katy that Catholic tradition forbids birth control because of the doctrine of natural law. Natural law was central to the writing of the Catholic theologian Thomas Aquinas. Judaism takes a different approach, that we cannot learn ethical behavior from nature. (The philosopher David Hume says the same thing, "you cannot learn an ought from an is.") Should nature be a source of ethics? If it is not, should birth control be permitted for a man? For a woman?

10. The Marital Bedroom – Many people believe that religion only permits sex between husband and wife in the classical missionary position. Rabbi Williams teaches that any sexual position is permissible, as long as it is playful and there is consent. Why did Judaism allow such a variety of sexual positions to a husband and wife? What do you believe should be forbidden between a husband and wife?

11. Laws of Family Purity – Rabbi Williams discusses the laws of family purity and *mikvah* with his class. These laws are widely practiced by Orthodox Jews but usually ignored by non-Orthodox Jews. Some feminists see these laws as patriarchal, because they consider a woman "unclean" during her menstrual period. Other feminists see these laws as positive, because each month there is a period where a man is forbidden to view his wife as a sexual object. Do you believe these laws can be interpreted in keeping with contemporary egalitarianism?

12. Jewish Mysticism – Rabbi Lebovic gives a sermon about theurgy, the ability of human activity to affect the cosmos. In particular, sex between a husband and wife with the proper attitude can bring the masculine and the feminine aspects of God together. Why did the mystics teach such an idea? Are there masculine and feminine aspects of the Divine, as the mystics teach? Or should we avoid speaking about gender when speaking of God?

13. Abortion – Those in the pro-life camp teach that human life begins at conception, and therefore abortion is murder. Those in the pro-choice camp teach that a developing fetus is part of a woman's body, and she should have absolute control over her own body. On the surface these two positions seem irreconcilable. Is there a compromise we can make in the abortion debate? What would a reasonable abortion law look like?

14. Gay Marriage – Rabbi Williams, who had been ambivalent until his final class, finally admits that he is willing to perform a gay marriage. Should clergy sanctify a marriage of a same sex couple? Was it appropriate for our culture to change the meaning of the word "marriage" to include same sex couples? Should Rabbi Williams seek permission of his synagogue board to perform such a marriage?

15. Confidentiality – Rabbi Williams promises confidentiality to his teenage students, unless they plan to harm themselves or others. This creates problems with the board of his synagogue. Should a rabbi or other clergy report conversations with minors to their parents? How can a rabbi or other clergy find the balance between their obligation to their students and their obligation to their congregation's board?

16. The Rabbi's Sex Class – Considering how the book ended, should Rabbi Williams have volunteered to teach this class? Why in the end did the school, his synagogue, and his wife object to the class? Is there anything Rabbi Williams could have done differently? Do you think he will teach such a class in his next congregation?

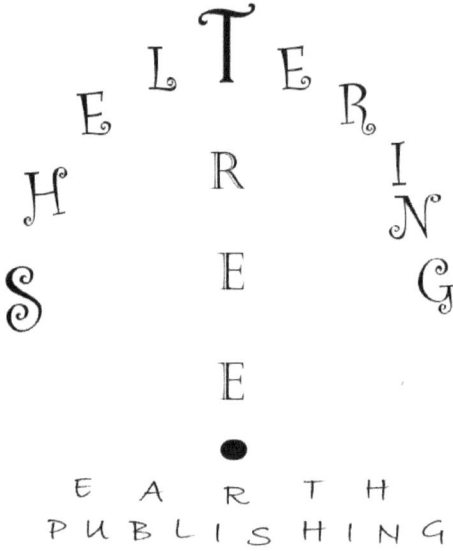

We are an exclusive traditional publishing house.

Our readers, once they finish one of our books, will be able to get up and face the world wiser, stronger, centered, and with the assurance that we are not alone: we are all a part of the Sheltering Tree on Earth.

If you as a writer feel that same calling, please refer to

ShelteringTree.Earth/writer-guidelines

www.ingramcontent.com/pod-product-compliance
Lightning Source LLC
Chambersburg PA
CBHW070923260626
47162CB00007B/2779